THE PANDEMONIUM OF PETS

A Love & Pets Christmas Romance, Book 7

A.G. HENLEY

Cover Designed by Najla Qamber Designs (www.najlaqamberdesigns.com)

Visit me at aghenley.com

Summary: A pet friendly Yuletide wedding goes disastrously, hilariously wrong.

CONTENTS

Hey, readers!

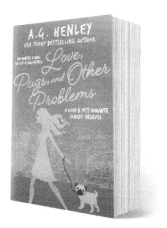

Get the FREE prequel ebook to the Love & Pets series, *Love, Pugs, and Other Problems,* an exclusive short story that tells how Amelia gets Doug the pug instead of a ring!

The PPP (The Pandemonium of Pets Playlist)

Check out the playlist of holiday songs I curated to go along with *The Pandemonium of Pets*.

Listen, read, and enjoy!

https://open.spotify.com/playlist/oEUQRCT5ci8htTqIRDAarL

Chapter One

IT'S BEGINNING TO LOOK A LOT LIKE CHRISTMAS

Travis

Amelia stands in front of the cabin window and looks out over the stunning Colorado mountains. She throws her arms wide as if to embrace the view.

"We're here. We made it. We're actually getting married in this gorgeous place."

I drop our bags on the floor and, puffy coat and winter hat still on, wrap my arms around her from behind. I can't wait to make this woman my wife.

Finally.

She rests her head against my chest. "Some days, I wasn't sure we would."

I kiss the top of her blonde hair. It's soft and smells like some kind of tropical bloom. "I'm sorry it's taken this long."

"It wasn't your fault. It wasn't anyone's fault. We were busy."

That's an understatement.

I'd met Amelia the year of the first annual Love & Pets party—the year my grandmother Jo died. We were engaged by year two, and now, too many years later, we're finally getting married. Tomorrow, to be exact. I tighten my arms around my fiancée.

Outside of the Lazy Dog Ranch's unofficial newlywed cabin, jokingly referred to by the staff as the Hitchin' Post, several feet of powdery snow glitter in the sun thanks to an early season blizzard a week ago. The cabin is a new addition to the ranch, built this past spring. Isa and Addie, clients of ours, had bought the ranch a few years ago, and Isa and her now husband Tobias, the ranch's head wrangler, had met shortly after. Addie and Isa originally shared the original owner's house up the hill, but since Isa and Tobias got married, Addie has her own place in another part of the ranch now.

Down the hill from us, Tobias strides toward the barn and stables, where a few of the ranch's main attractions—the horses —stand in a snow-covered field, blankets on their backs. The equines are the stars at this dude ranch, but Addie, Isa, and Tobias make the place what it is: a warm and welcoming family vacation spot. They'd been great to work with as we planned this holiday wedding shindig.

Amelia turns and presses herself up on her toes to kiss me. "I can't imagine a more blissful setting to exchange our vows."

Her blue-green eyes never fail to capture me; eyes that I've loved for years, through the happiest of times and the hardest.

Together, we'd built our Love & Pets veterinary practice to be the most successful mobile clinic in Colorado, and we're expanding soon to a second vehicle. We have more patients than we know what to do with, many of whom are arriving today to join in the festivities. But Amelia had also been there for me when I'd lost Jo, my only real family. That was one of the roughest times in my life.

"We could have signed the legal paperwork any old day." I'd offered to many times, in fact, so that we didn't have to wait to be married.

"I'm so glad we didn't. Now, we can afford to have a big,

beautiful wedding, lots of guests, and all the wonderful memories it will bring for years to come."

I caress her pink cheek, her fleecy hair, her long neck. My hand trails to her shoulders, then to her back, and I pull her against me. As my lips find hers, a whine drags our attention away.

"What is it, Doug?" Amelia asks. One of our two pugs lies in the crate we'd brought, his head on his paws. "I don't think he's feeling well," Amelia says frowning. "He didn't eat well yesterday or today, and I haven't seen him poop in a while."

When you work with animals like we do, talking about poop in the same breath as a kiss comes with the territory.

Daisy, our other pug, licks her snowy paws beside Doug, her stomach bulging. "Looks like Daisy might be snarfing his food."

Amelia snorts. "I wouldn't be surprised if he offers it to her on a silver platter."

I laugh. Dougie is an adoring romantic partner—if you can call a neutered male and spayed female romantic partners.

"We can take a look at him in a minute," I say. "But I'm not quite finished here." I bring her body into mine again, enjoying the way we fit together in all the right places.

I wasn't being noble before. As much as I'm looking forward to our long-awaited celebration with friends and family, I could do without any of the pomp and circumstance this weekend. I just want Amelia to be my wife.

Now. This minute. Yesterday. Always.

I press my lips to hers again with more urgency, lift her off of her feet, and move toward the bed—when the door slams open. The dogs leap to their feet.

"I mean it. If you tell Amelia that, I will never speak to you again."

Avery, Amelia's older sister, backs into the room holding a bucket of champagne and a plate of chocolate-covered strawberries wrapped in plastic. She's petite with short blonde hair and, currently, an angry expression on her face.

Avery is followed by their mother, Joyce, a thin woman who looks like an older version of Amelia: blonde, fair, and small-boned. But that's where the similarity ends between my fiancée and her parent, in my experience.

"I just think she's *crazy* to be getting married, after what we all went through at your father's hands."

Amelia withers, like a flower exposed to its first frost. I put an arm around her and clear my throat. Avery whirls at the sound.

"Oh! We thought you two would already be down at the lodge. Well, that's one surprise ruined." She holds up the bucket and plate and then sets them on a small table near the cabin's mini kitchen. "Happy day before your wedding!"

"Thank you very much," I say. "How are you today, Joyce?"

Joyce's eyes narrow and her lips thin. I can practically sniff out her disapproval from across the room. It smells a lot like expensive perfume. "I'm fine. Thank you, Travis." She turns her attention to her younger daughter. "Amelia, you aren't planning to wear *that* tonight, are you?"

"I, well . . ." She looks down at her white sweater, dark jeans, and cowboy boots, and shrivels a little more. "It's only a casual barbecue for our guests, Mom."

Avery's eyes flash at their mother. "You look gorgeous, Melly. Love that outfit."

Joyce ignores her older daughter. "Well, you could have made a bit more effort. And you'll drip sauce all over that top. Mark my words."

Daisy sniffs Joyce's pant leg suspiciously, and Joyce pushes her —not hard, but still—out of her way with her foot to get to the fridge, where she stores the wine and berries.

Amelia and Avery's eyes lock, speaking volumes behind their mother's back. None of the volumes are complimentary. I haven't had the . . . pleasure . . . of spending much time with Joyce over the years. A holiday here or there, and a few visits from her that Amelia mostly tried to shield me from. But I haven't needed a lot of time to take her measure.

"So, Amelia, is Dad coming?" Avery asks her sister pointedly. Amelia winces.

Joyce whirls. "Michael's coming? I thought he wasn't coming!"

Amelia shrugs meekly. "I'm not sure. You know Dad."

"I can't believe he's coming," Joyce says. "Why did you even invite him, Amelia?"

"Because he's our father, that's why," Avery answers. "And he'll be walking you down the aisle if he does come, right Mel?"

Amelia hems and haws, obviously not wanting to upset her mother. Which is the exact opposite of what Avery's comment was intended to do.

"I'm not sure yet. Kenny offered to escort me, too."

"I love Kenny," Avery says with affection. "He and Ruston were in the lobby checking in before we came up."

"We could walk down," Amelia says to me quickly. "It would be fun to see people as they arrive. More time to visit."

Doug and Daisy rush toward the door, barking, at the word *walk*. Joyce hustles out of their way as if they might give her ticks and fleas in passing.

"Yes, you can go too." Amelia croons to the dogs.

"And another thing. Why on earth did you invite people to bring their pets?" Joyce complains. "You might as well have chosen the zoo as your venue."

This time, Avery looks like she agrees with their mother, even if she won't say so in front of her.

I field this one. "Pets are what we do. They're a huge part of our lives, and we wanted our patients and their owners to be able to share in the fun with us this weekend."

Amelia and I have worked hard to build our business, and we couldn't have done it without the support and referrals of our clients. Inviting them and their pets is a way we can thank them for helping us succeed.

Joyce tosses her shoulder-length hair back. It moves in one fascinating clump. "Ridiculous, if you ask me. But it's your wedding."

Amelia bristles, but I can tell she's not going to argue. She's been working on building some assertiveness with their mother for a long time, but . . . she isn't quite there yet. After snapping a leash on Doug and grabbing her coat, she marches out of the cabin.

With a heavy sigh, her mother follows. And after a sad shake of her head in my direction, Avery leaves, too.

Daisy waits expectantly by her own leash. I move that way. I miss my grandma Jo every single day, so I'm happy to have any and all of Amelia's family members in our lives. But I can't help thinking that Joyce would give any monster-in-law a run for her money.

Families fight and argue at weddings and especially around the holidays, right? If that's true, then . . . it's beginning to look a lot like Christmas.

Chapter Two

SOMEONE IS MISSING AT CHRISTMAS

Amelia

My heart is full of candy canes, peppermint kisses, and more than a few red hots because Travis and I are finally getting married!

But the excitement that has trailed glittery fingers all over my skin for months falls away as Doug and I tread carefully down the snowy pathway from the Hitchin' Post to the lodge and across the Kissing Bridge—a charming wooden structure that spans the now frozen creek running right through the middle of the ranch. Avery and Mom follow, still bickering.

It's a dream to have Avery, her long-time boyfriend Jason, and a bunch of our friends and clients here to celebrate. If only my mother *wasn't* here. I try to remember why I'd invited her.

Oh yes, because Travis had asked me to. He wants to start our marriage right by including as much family as we can. Including Mom.

I shake my head as she picks her way across the wooden slats of the bridge in her high heeled boots. Why did she wear those things to a mountain wedding? I'd made it clear it was going to be a casual weekend, right down to my beautiful, simple wedding dress. One of our clients, a talented seamstress, offered to design and make it for me after Travis and I surgically removed an elastic hair tie from the stomach of her American Shorthair cat, Coco.

"I hate the snow. And the cold," Mom grumbles.

Avery scoffs. "Mom, you live in Kansas City. It gets snowy and cold too."

Mom raises a carefully shaped eyebrow at my sister. "*That's* how I know I hate it."

I take a deep, centering breath, let them pass me, and then wait in the middle of the bridge for Travis and Daisy to catch up. When they do, I put my arms around my fiancé. The bridge has been the site of many first kisses and proposals, we'd been told. It's legendary.

"I'm not sure I can deal with Mom being here," I whisper in his ear. "Her complaining is like a rusty nail scratching down my spine."

Travis runs his fingers lightly up and down my back.

I sigh and close my eyes. "Ooh, I like that, though."

"Good. There will be plenty more where that came from later." He lifts my chin and kisses me softly on the lips.

I gaze into his dark brown, almost black eyes. His wavy dark curls escape from under his winter cap, brushing his shoulders, and he has a hint of scruff. He could shave twice a day and still have a hint of scruff after a few hours. He's so handsome.

"Having your mom here will be a good memory one day. I promise."

"How do you know?"

"I don't . . . but I sure wish my mom and Jo could be here, despite everything."

I hug him fiercely, hoping to ease the hurt I know he's feeling. Although I'd only known Josephine for a short time before she passed away, she'd made a big impression. She was an amazing woman, full of energy until the very end and totally devoted to Travis and to the success of his fledgling veterinary practice. Travis' mom had died years before that, and he never knew his father.

He tugs the zipper of my winter coat up an inch. "Anyway, I think we should make the best of having your family here."

"Amelia!" Mom screeches from the open doors of the lodge, waving frantically. "You have guests here to see you!"

"The best of it, huh?" I raise an eyebrow at Travis.

He smiles and takes my free hand. "Host and hostess time."

"I don't mind that, either," I say as we walk on.

"Good thing. I have a feeling we're going to be doing plenty of it."

We follow Mom through the polished wood front doors and into the two-story lobby of the main lodge, where I immediately spot familiar faces. "Oh! There's Bea and Seb! And Stevie and Logan!"

Several clients and friends stand at the reception desk inside, waiting their turn to check in. Beatrix holds a pet carrier that I know from experience houses a sweet tuxedo cat named Fluffernutter, one of her and Sebastian's many, many rescue felines. Stevie and Logan have their border collie, Bean, on a short leash. Bean's tail wags furiously as she watches people and pets meander around the lobby. I head that way, but someone grabs and hugs me before I get far.

"Hi, Bridezilla!" a man says teasingly.

"Ruston! You made it!"

"Indeed, we did." Ruston, a stout guy in his early thirties, is wrapped in a red cashmere scarf and plaid winter coat. His outerwear screams the holidays. He hands me a gorgeous bouquet full of gardenias, irises, and white roses plus tons of greenery. Florists give the most glorious gifts.

"Oh, these are beautiful!" I stuff my face into them and inhale.

"The arrangements for the reception will be delivered tomorrow."

I hug him again. "Thank you so much for creating them."

"I wish you'd have let me go bigger and bolder—"

I shake my head and smile. "Simple is what we want. Where's Kenny?"

"Present," a man says from my elbow. "And accounted for. How are you, Princess?"

I smother him with a hug. Kenny was my coworker and reluctant partner in crime way back when I worked at the dubious law firm of Hart, Hand, & Butz before I went back to school to become a veterinary technician.

When I finally pull away to look at the thin, conservatively dressed black man in front of me, I frown. "Are you okay, Kenny? You look tired."

"Have you ever heard the expression 'burning the midnight oil'?"

I squint and shake my head.

"It means you don't get much sleep. That's the life of a newly minted practicing attorney."

"Max never worked that hard," I say, referring to our old coworker, a young, hot, jerk of a lawyer.

"That is because Max was a piss poor attorney," Kenny says matter-of-factly. Ruston snorts and greets Travis, who's come over after saying hi to Bea, Seb, Stevie, and Logan. I pat Kenny's chest. "I hope you can relax and get some sleep while you're here. How's your mom and Chi-Chi?"

"Lord help me. Driving us crazy. I thought I'd have to bring that dog up here with us when Mother went to help my great-aunt Martha after she took a fall. But nothing was broken, so everyone's back home."

"We would have loved for Chi to come!" I say.

"Well, we wouldn't," Kenny says, and I laugh. Kenny never has been a big fan of his mother's chihuahua mixes. "Now you go on and greet your other guests." He lowers his voice. "But I do want to meet *your* mother at some point. Is she in good form?"

I groan. "Perfect form."

He rubs his hands together and smiles, a rare sight, and he and Ruston head in the direction of the bar around the corner from reception.

Travis and I turn to welcome other guests, but I'm distracted by Isa and Addie. They stand with their heads together. Isa's hair is a smooth, dark sheet halfway down her back, while Addie's is a sunny blonde long bob. When they see me looking, their expressions brighten from concerned to casual, although I can tell it's a show. Uh oh. They come our way.

"Hey, Amelia, Travis! How are things going so far?" Addie's voice is as cheerful as ever, but I hear the worry—no, make that borderline panic—behind it.

"What is it?" I ask. "What's happened?" I glance at Travis; his eyes are narrowed with unease.

"Now, please don't worry, um, too much." Isa's expression is a little calmer than Addie's. "But, well, do you know that man over there? He's one of your guests."

She points down to the far end of the lobby. A man in a hoodie and jeans, his hands thrust in his front pockets and a backpack on his back, stands between the absolutely enormous, elaborately decorated Christmas tree and the lit and roaring fireplace. I exchange a second, more troubled glance with Travis.

"Brent," we say at the same time.

Brent is a close second on the list of people I'm not so sure we should've invited. But again, Travis had talked me into it. Brent had hit a rough patch for a while there, including some jail time, but he's been doing a lot better. Everyone deserves second chances, Travis always says.

"Well, he told us something we thought you should know, although we don't plan to share the information widely," Isa says with a pinched expression.

"What?" I ask again, dread filling my previously peppermint kissed heart.

"His . . . pet is missing," Isa says.

"His pet? Severus the Second?" I clutch Travis' arm. "That means—"

Addie shudders, and then nods. "There's a five-foot-long boa constrictor loose somewhere in the lodge."

Chapter Three

ALL I WANT FOR CHRISTMAS IS YOU

Travis

"How did he get out?" Amelia asks in a soft wail.

Addie looks as worried as Amelia sounds. "His owner—Brent?—is staying in one of the new rooms here in the lodge. He apparently slithered right out of his cage while Brent was out on his balcony for a few minutes."

Isa, Addie, and Tobias had added a wing of guest rooms to this main building as alternative lodging to the cabins that the ranch has always offered to guests. The rooms are great for weddings like ours, and other events, too, when guests don't need the space of a cabin. Brent must have booked one for himself and his wedding guest . . . which sounds like it might be Sev Two. I know this is supposed to be serious, but I can't help chuckling.

Amelia gapes at me. "Are you . . . laughing?"

I try to hide my mirth. "I'll go help Brent look for him."

She turns to me and lowers her voice while Isa and Addie

hurry away to help with the streams of guests arriving to check in. "Travis. We agreed. You *promised*."

I take her hand. "I know. I'll be gone for ten minutes tops."

Early on in the wedding planning, when we decided to invite our guests to bring their pets to the ranch, we also promised each other that we would *not* be on call for any pet emergencies over the weekend.

A new emergency veterinary practice opened only a fifteen-minute drive away, twenty tops. If there are problems, which I honestly don't anticipate, our guests can take their pets there. But this isn't a veterinary emergency, it's a client and friend who's lost his pet. Even though his pet happens to be a fifty-pound snake, Brent must be worried.

"It'll be worth the lost time if Brent and I find Sev Two right now instead of some other unsuspecting guest—like your mother."

Amelia sucks in a breath and glances at Joyce, who's speaking to one of our colleagues, a vet with a practice near our house. She's gesturing our way animatedly. Who knows what she's telling her.

Amelia kisses me. "Okay. Ten minutes. Then you'll be back, right?"

"Right." I touch my forehead to hers. "Did I tell you how beautiful you look today? And how much I can't wait to be your husband?"

She smiles. "I think you did."

"Well it's true. Don't listen to your mom. Don't listen to anyone who tells you otherwise. You're an amazing woman with so many gifts, and I can't believe my good luck that you're about to be mine."

She puts a hand on my cheek. "You know I feel exactly the same about you. And as much as it frustrates me sometimes, I love your good heart the most. I realize you can't ignore a friend who needs help, but remember, we have *lots* of friends here this weekend. We need time to visit with them all, and I'd like us to have a little time together, too."

"I'll be back before you know it."

I walk via the edge of the room, rather than right through the middle, to avoid getting caught by too many of the arriving guests. Thankfully, most of them are on the other side of the lobby checking in and then going on to their rooms to unpack and get ready for the barbecue tonight. Which is in—I check my watch—exactly an hour and a half. There's some breathing room.

After shaking hands quickly with several friends and saying hello over the din of barking dogs, meowing cats, and the chatter of humans, I reach Brent. He's gazing out of the floor-to-almost-ceiling wall of windows. This side of the lobby features a river rock fireplace, lots of comfortable leather couches and chairs for gathering, and of course the two-story Christmas tree. It looms over Brent's head, sparkling with the white, gold, and silver decorations Isa and Addie adorned it with. Wrapped gifts sit under the tree labeled to Amelia and me.

"Brent," I hold out my hand to shake his. "How are you, man?"

"Good, good." He seems distracted.

"How are things at work?" I'd helped him get started with his training to be a veterinary assistant, and now he works at a friend's practice in Denver.

"Yeah, going fine." His eyes shift from me to the crowd of people behind me, not settling on anyone.

"That's great." I thrust my hands in my jeans' pockets. "So . . . I heard you lost something."

He squints. "Lost something? No. Oh—you heard about Sev Two? He's around somewhere."

I grit my teeth. I try not to judge people, but Brent can be hard work sometimes. "Don't you think we should look for him? Amelia and I would rather he be safe in your room instead of, er, checking out other accommodations. You know I like snakes, but not everyone does."

"Yeah," he sighs. "You're probably right. I was waiting for Sarah and Ben to show up, then I thought I'd look around for him before dinner."

Sarah and Ben are also clients of ours and friends of Brent's. They'd all met in a pet grief group a while ago. In fact, Amelia and I had met Brent through them.

"Let's take a look around for him now so he doesn't get too far. Then we'll come back. Sarah and Ben will text you when they get here anyway, won't they?"

"Probably. Okay."

"Great—so, where's your room? Maybe we should start there."

"It's up on the second floor." He turns toward the elevators, so I follow him.

"What do you think of the ranch?" I ask once we reach them.

He punches the up button. "It's nice. Good choice, bro."

"What did you decide to do tomorrow?" The ranch is offering a couple of activities for our guests like snowshoeing and cross-country skiing.

"I thought I'd go to the pool."

I stare at him as the elevator doors open. "The pool? Is it open?" It can't be more than forty degrees outside.

He side eyes me. "It was a joke."

I blink. "Right." With Brent, you can never tell.

As the doors open to the second floor, a screaming woman pushes past us to get inside. I vaguely recognize her as one of Amelia's college friends whom I met maybe two years ago when she visited from somewhere out East.

I take her arm to steady her. Her blue eyes are wide, and she's pale.

"Are you okay?" I ask.

"No! There's a giant snake in the hallway!"

"Cool. Which way did he go?" Brent asks. He steps out and glances left and right down the hallway.

She gives him a look like she's questioning his sanity. "I didn't ask him! I ran!"

"I'm sorry he scared you," I say calmly. "Severus is Brent's pet, and we're looking for him."

"And he's harmless," Brent says derisively.

"Maybe to *you*. *I* almost peed my pants." The words spit out like nails from a nail gun.

"Listen, I know you've had a shock, but if you could keep this to yourself, we're going to find the snake right now," I say. "There's no reason to alarm people—"

"No reason to alarm people? There's a snake as big as my first car somewhere in this hotel! You can bet your Christmas pudding I'll be telling everyone I see to be on the lookout for that monster!"

As she slams a manicured finger against the close door button, I jump back into the hallway and the doors shut, separating me from her narrowed eyes and crossed arms. I'm sure I'll hear about this later from Amelia. Unless her friend didn't recognize me? Probably wishful thinking.

"I'll go this way, you go that way," I say to Brent, pointing one way down the hallway and then the other. "When you get to the end, turn around and we'll meet back here. Shout if you see him. Sound good?"

"Yep." He turns, and hands in pockets, wanders down the hallway whistling off tune a Christmas song that had been playing in the lobby. I shake my head and turn the other way. This shouldn't be hard. Find Sev, put him back in whatever enclosure Brent brought for him, and get back to Amelia's side. Oh, and calm the panic.

As I look left and right, passing room doors, I realize I'm a little relieved to be up here instead of down there. I love Amelia, and I'd meant every word I'd said about marrying her whenever and however she chose, but I'd also meant it when I said I wouldn't mind a ceremony with just the two of us and a preacher.

Despite the fact that I argued for several outliers to be invited, making the guest list even longer.

I'm not the most social guy in the world, which Amelia says she doesn't mind. But sometimes I wonder. Will I make her happy in the long run? Will she get tired of our life of work and more work, driving around the Denver metro area looking after sick animals, attending pet-centered charity and other events, and organizing the annual Love & Pets party, which is becoming a bigger and more complicated beast every year? Does anyone know the answers to these kinds of questions before they get married??

I check every nook and cranny between the elevators and the end of the hall. No Sev Two. But as I reach the emergency exit door, I spy a housekeeping room with its door partially cracked. I push it open. Inside, rolling laundry carts sit full of clean and folded bed sheets, towels, and the odd plush bathrobe that the ranch provides to guests. I wouldn't think much of it except for one thing . . . the small pile of snake feces sitting beside one of the carts.

Fortunately or unfortunately, however you want to look at it, I know exactly what boa constrictor droppings look like.

I hesitate. I'm not all that thrilled to dive inside the carts of laundry to find Sev Two. Plus, I don't have time. My ten minutes is almost up. I jog back down the hall, find Brent, and tell him what I'd found.

"Listen, I have to get back downstairs now, but at least you know where he is, right?" I say. "Head down there and search the room and let me know when you find him."

"Yep, I'm on it." Brent strolls back that way, still whistling, still in no hurry.

Laughing to myself, I get on the elevator while wondering what chaos I'll find after Amelia's friend spreads the word about a massive escaped snake in the hotel.

You can bet your Christmas pudding I already know.

Chapter Four

MERRY CHRISTMAS FROM THE FAMILY

Amelia

I cover my face with dismay. No, no, no, no, no. This is the last thing we need.

"And then it slithered right past me and down the hallway!" My college friend, Catherine, regales a group of our guests with the story of how she faced down a giant snake in the hallway. To hear her tell it, Sev Two had been a deadly fire-breathing dragon and she was the princess locked in the tower who'd saved herself from the beast.

Across the lobby, Isa and Addie look like they're already regretting allowing pets at the ranch at all, much less for our wedding.

"A snake?" My mother's voice is shrill. "Amelia? Did you hear this? Apparently, someone has lost a *snake* in the hotel."

I hold up my hands placatingly. "I heard the news, but listen, Severus is harmless," mostly, "and his owner and Travis are upstairs capturing him right now." I hope. "Please don't worry."

"Don't worry?" If Mom's voice rises any higher, she'll shatter the lodge's beautiful windows. "Don't worry? How can we possibly not worry?"

"It's easy, Mother. You put it out of your mind and enjoy your youngest daughter's wedding weekend." The sarcasm in Avery's voice is as thick as overcooked mashed potatoes.

"It's a snake, Avery," Mom says. They're practically toe to toe. Our guests stare and I can almost see the news about Sev Two, er, snaking around the room. I exchange a helpless glance with Jason. Over the years he's been with Avery, he's learned more than he wanted to know about our challenges with our mother. He steps in, bless him.

"Joyce, let me get you another drink and walk you to your room. I'll check it out and make sure there's no snake in there." Unfortunately, Mom's staying here in the lodge and not in one of the cabins where I'm fairly certain Severus the Second is not.

"Thank you, Jason. That would make me feel so much better. *You're* such a gentleman."

Gallantly, Jason offers his arm and Mom takes it. Avery shakes her head dismissively at Mom's comment, but a little of the joy drains out of me. I know perfectly well who she's comparing Jason to in her head. Travis.

I'm guessing Mom will never approve of him, simply because he'll be my husband; she isn't exactly a fan of the institution of marriage. And he's not from what she'd call a "good" family. She's said many times that she doesn't like his longer than average hair or his casual personal style or the many animals we keep at our home. As if those things make a man a good or bad husband.

I push Mom out of my thoughts and turn to welcome a newly arrived guest and client who thankfully didn't bring our patient, her chatty cockatiel Lolita. But as I do, the sound of a deep voice spins me around.

"Hello, girls."

My father, Michael, stands behind me with his wife, Suzanne, their bags in hand.

"Dad—thanks for coming." Tentatively, I hug him and shake

my stepmother's hand. Although they've been married for years, we've never been close.

I glance over my shoulder toward the elevator. My sister's looking the same way. Thankfully, Mom's gone. This little reunion will happen one way or another, but I'd much rather it be without her as a witness. She'd only use it against us later. And where is Travis? It's definitely been ten minutes.

I turn my attention to Dad. His dark blonde hair sports patches of gray at the temples, and more wrinkles and sunspots line and dot his face than the last time I saw him, but he's still trim and dressed as impeccably as ever in jeans, boots, a crisp white button-down, and a sport coat. A wool winter coat and cashmere scarf hangs over his arm.

Suzanne looks nice, too, wearing winter white pants, sensible but fashionable boots, and a navy coat, but . . . she also looks thinner and paler than I remember.

"How was your trip here?" I ask after they say hello to Avery. My sister's greeting is as cool and smooth as whipped cream on a pumpkin pie.

"Fine, fine. Easy flight from Chicago," our father says. "We got lucky with the weather—"

"I could have sworn I put my key in my purse . . ." Mom's shrill voice cuts through the conversations filling the lobby. I flinch and curse to myself. She's back. And a quick glance tells me she's seen Dad. After a slight pause, she beelines to us.

"Well, if it isn't the father of the bride," Mom says. "Welcome to your daughters' lives, Michael."

Dad stiffens. When he speaks, he lowers his voice compared to hers. It's not hard to do. "Hello, Joyce. You look well."

Avery steps to my side protectively, and out of the corner of my eye, I spot Travis coming around the corner from the elevator. Relief flows through me. I need his support for this showdown.

"Thank you. I'm surprised you noticed."

"Of course, I noticed. You've always been a beautiful woman. You just weren't a great wife," Dad says mildly.

"Dad," Avery and I say warningly at the same time.

"Oh, that's rich," Mom says. "You're the one who cheated with every floozy you met on your," she makes finger quotes, "business trips." She stares poisonously at Suzanne, who has her hand on my father's arm as if to lead him away. All around us, people quiet, watching the family circus.

"Dad," Avery jumps in with a rush. "You haven't seen Jason in a while. Why don't you come with me and we can catch up?"

She throws me an apologetic look and leads our father and stepmother across the lobby to where Jason managed to hide when he saw what was about to go down with our parents. He steps out from behind the Christmas tree now to shake their hands. I thank Avery silently for her interference. That could have easily gotten even uglier, although it was bad enough.

"Did you *hear* that?" Catherine asks her husband, Tom, in a not-so-quiet whisper. All around me, the news about Sev Two turns to whispering about my parents' mini-fight. More than a few pitying looks are thrown my way.

"Hey, love, everything okay?" Travis asks.

Um, no, love. There's a snake missing inside our wedding venue and my parents had a fight in front of half our guests within one minute of seeing each other again. But I can't say anything, because Mom's still here.

"Travis, can you please take Mom up to her room and make sure Sev Two isn't in there?" I ask with a widening of my eyes that says I *really* need him to do this for me.

Mom sniffs haughtily, like of course Travis would be honored to escort her. "First, I need to get a new room key. I've lost mine."

"Of course," Travis says politely.

Have I mentioned how much I love this man? I grab his hand and whisper, "Did you find Sev Two?"

"In a way. Brent's on his trail." He plants a kiss in my palm and follows Mom to the desk.

"Amelia!" A new voice catches my attention. It's Sarah, a client and librarian up in Fort Collins, her husband Ben, and their young Labrador retriever, Max. Sarah has him on a short leash as he strains to greet me, tail wagging. He barks loudly, so I kneel to pet him.

"Hey, you three," I say, glad for the distraction. "I'm so glad you could make it. The last time we saw you was, when?"

Sarah groans. "About six months ago when Max sliced his foot on the metal hedge divider."

"How did I forget? He left bloody footprints all over your condo." It had been like a canine crime scene. They'd tried to clean it up, treat it, and bandage it, but his paw kept bleeding, so they called us. Thankfully, it had only needed a few stitches.

"It's great to see you when it's not an emergency or involving shots or thermometers up the rectum," Ben says with a wink as he kisses my cheek. "Where's Doctor Travis?"

"Dealing with my mother," I say in an undertone.

"Uh oh, fireworks already?" Sarah asks with compassion. Her brown curly hair falls into her eyes, and she sweeps it away. She's dressed adorably as always in knee-high boots and a turtleneck dress under her open winter coat.

"I'm extremely glad you missed it. Oh, and listen, not to saddle you with this the second you walk in the door, but . . . Brent."

Sarah groans. "What? What did he do?"

"He's lost Severus the Second."

Ben's green eyes go wide. "Here?"

"Somewhere in the lodge. Can I impose on you two to help look for him? Travis tried, but they haven't found him yet. I think Brent's still looking for him up on the second floor."

"Of course," Sarah says. "Let us check in and drop our stuff off in our room, and then we'll be happy to help."

"I'll get in line at the desk," Ben tells her.

"Thank you." She kisses him, and he kisses her back, then

whispers something in her ear that makes her blush. It's so nice to see how in love they are. They'd had a rocky path to the altar.

Max paws lightly at my knee, so I pet him again. His fur is still soft like a puppy, and he practically laughs with his brown eyes and lolling pink tongue. He's more of an adolescent now, but he still has a puppyish attitude.

Of course, as soon as I let him go, he sniffs my crotch. Like I said: an adolescent. Suddenly, his nose lifts into the air, and he pulls Sarah hard to her right, dragging her across the room.

Daisy and Doug are in the capable hands of my teenaged cousin, Bethany, who flew in last night from Kansas with my aunt and uncle. They're all standing in the sitting area by the fireplace talking to a friend of Travis' named Billy, who holds his female schnauzer mix, Skye.

With fierce determination, Max drags Sarah toward them. She fights him, but he's so focused, she finally gives up and allows him to greet the other dogs while she meets the humans. After a few seconds, Sarah gasps loud enough to be heard across the room.

"Max, no! Stop that!"

The young Lab is, well, making advances on Skye. The joyful abandon with which he's trying to have his way is hilarious on the one hand and horrible on the other. Skye rushes away from him, while Sarah does her best to pull Max back. And that's when I remember that our passionate patient is due to be neutered when we get back from our honeymoon.

Laughter erupts across the lobby, accompanied by a few disapproving looks. Sarah is pink-faced and apologetic.

I check my watch. We've already had a missing boa constrictor, the first round of a prize fight between my parents, and a display of erotic romance—doggy style—and there's still an hour before the welcome barbecue.

Surely all of the things that could go wrong this weekend now have.

Surely.

Chapter Five
ALL I WANT FOR CHRISTMAS (IS MY TWO FRONT TEETH)

Travis

"Are you ready?"

Amelia's in the bathroom of our cabin, touching up her makeup. Or something along those lines. I don't know half the stuff women do to themselves when they're getting ready to be seen, but whatever my fiancée does is pure magic. She steps out of the bathroom radiating health and happiness. I take a second to admire her.

She has on the same outfit as before, but her hair, previously in a ponytail, now lays over her shoulders, glittering gold in the last of the sunset leaking through the windows. Her blue eyes sparkle, her lips are as pink and soft as shades of a Western sunset, and the engagement ring on her finger sparkles.

"You're beautiful. I love you," I say.

Her smile widens as she looks me over. "So are you."

I'd taken a few minutes to change into a nice pair of jeans, a navy and green plaid shirt, and better boots for the cold. We'll be outside tonight, albeit with a fire pit, coats, and hot spiked beverages. Luckily, the temperature still hovers around forty degrees, so hopefully not cold enough to frostbite anyone who didn't come prepared for the weather.

I pull Amelia into my arms to kiss her, but my cell phone rings so loud that Doug and Daisy bark and we jump. I keep her close as I pull the phone out of my pocket and glare at it.

"What now?" I mutter. "Hey, Addie, what's up?" My voice is a littler sharper than I mean for it to be.

"Hi, Travis, I'm sorry to bother you. I know you two are probably getting ready for the barbecue." She sounds worried again.

I sigh. Yes, and trying to get a proper kiss in. "That's all right. How can I help?"

I ask that a lot. It's a standard question for clients, inviting them to tell me more about their pets' problems than the line or two I get when they make an appointment. The animals can't help when they have health issues, of course. But sometimes I want the humans to solve their own problems, you know?

There's a dramatic moan from the background of Addie's side of the call. "We've had a small accident in the kitchen. It's one of our assistants—not Wanda, who you met—but Myra. I was wondering . . . are any of your guests doctors or nurses?"

"I don't think so."

"Oh. Okay." She hesitates but I feel a question coming, and my heart sinks. "Travis, I know you're a veterinarian and not a human doctor, but would you mind taking a look at her? Kind of to, maybe, triage?"

I hesitate. Amelia gives me a questioning look. "I, uh, I'd love to help, but like you said—"

"I know it's wrong to ask, and normally I'd drive her to the urgent care like usual—"

Like usual? How often does this Myra person get injured?

"But we're a little short-staffed in the kitchen tonight because Mateo called in sick, and Tobias is sorting something out in the barn so Isa's on her own getting the patio set up for the barbecue. She needs my help, but so does Myra—"

I shake my head at the dizzying array of names. "Let me see what I can do. Is Myra still down in the kitchen?"

"Yes. Thank you *so* much!"

"I'll be right there."

Amelia tilts her head as I hang up. "What is it?"

I hold up my hands. "Okay, first of all, it's not a veterinary emergency, so technically I'm not breaking my promise. One of Isa and Addie's kitchen staff has had an accident and they're short-staffed, so they need me to take a look."

"Is that legal?" Amelia asks.

"Probably not. But I'm not planning on doing any treatment. I don't even know what happened yet." I squint. "This is a poor idea, isn't it?"

"Yes, but I love that you always want to help."

She kisses me, letting her lips settle against mine long enough to drive me crazy.

"C'mon, I'll go with you." Amelia puts the dogs into their crate—no pets allowed at meals, plus it will be too cold for them outside—and pulls on her heavy puffer coat followed by thick gloves. I do the same, then yank a navy wool beanie over my head.

Amelia touches my hair. "You look like a little boy with your curls poking out under that hat."

"Hopefully a little boy you want to kiss?" I pause. "Wait, that didn't sound right. Never mind, let's go find Myra."

The ranch at night is almost as magical as the ranch during the day. Isa, Addie, and Tobias had strung buckets of white lights around the rooflines of every cabin, the lodge, the barn, some of the fencing for the horses, and even across the Kissing Bridge. The soft glow against the crisp layer of snow on the ground is truly charming. I really want to stop and make out with Amelia on the bridge, but . . . duty calls.

We pick our way along the path to the side door of the

kitchen. We know the layout of the property pretty well thanks to visits to see Zip, Zap, and Zoom, the three resident ranch dachshunds, and of course from our trips here to decide on menus and that kind of thing during the wedding planning. The kitchen is in the lodge, adjacent to the dining room, where the reception will be tomorrow evening.

And it's hopping. The head chef Wanda, a tall and generously sized white-haired woman, stirs an absolutely enormous pot while barking orders to two very young-looking assistants, one male and one female, who scurry to do her bidding. "Tallulah, get the rolls in the oven! Owen, check the meat again on the grill."

Addie stands beside a seated brown-haired woman in a white chef's shirt and black pants whose head rests on the back of her chair with an ice pack on her mouth.

Addie hops up. "Thank you so much for coming. I'm not sure what to do."

The woman, who's about thirty-five I'd say, lifts her head up, her brown eyes bleary, and opens her mouth. Her top lip is puffy, her two front teeth are bloody, and one's crooked. I'm instantly suspicious; she looks like she was punched.

"Hi, Myra," I say, "I'm Travis and this is Amelia. Can I take a closer look at your mouth?"

"Hi, Doc," she slurs as if she doesn't want to move her lips much. "Thanks for coming. I can't believe I did this tonight of all nights. I guess tomorrow night would have been worse, but tonight was bad enough." As she chatters, specks of blood splatter on her white top.

Myra glances sidelong at Wanda as she speaks, who shakes her head even though her back is turned to us.

My eyes narrow. "What happened?"

"I, uh, I ran into one of the pans hanging from the rack."

Myra points to a rack mounted on the ceiling with cast iron pots and pans hanging from them. It's hard to see how she could have run into one with her face when a large stainless-steel work-table stands directly under them.

"I think you're going to need to be seen by an actual doctor. Or probably more specifically a dentist. But, why don't you come with me to the bathroom where we can clean up your mouth a little so I can see better. Is there a staff bathroom we can use?" I ask Addie. No need to upset the guests.

"Right back here."

Addie leads Myra, Amelia, and me toward the large pantry and refrigerated room behind the kitchen. A small restroom is visible at the end of the hallway.

"I'll give you some privacy." Addie pats Myra on the arm as she leaves.

Wanda, I'd noticed, kept glaring at Myra as we spoke in the kitchen, but she'd had her hands full at the stovetop. Guests are probably already gathering in the lobby, ready to be fed and watered, and the kitchen staff looked tense. Can't say I feel much different.

As soon as Addie walks away, I ask Myra to carefully wash out her mouth with water, and then I gently examine her front teeth. They bleed a little, and they wiggle a lot.

"Myra," I ask quietly. "What really happened? I don't believe you did this running into a pan." I glance at Amelia, who looks alarmed.

Myra lowers her eyes. "No, I didn't."

I wait, but she doesn't say anything else.

"Were you . . . hit?" I ask. "Did Wanda, or someone else, do this?"

Myra's eyes open wide. She sputters, sending droplets of blood flying, then laughs. "No! No. Wanda is my mother-in-law. She'd never do that. But I . . ." Her words come out in a blood-specked stream. "I'm always doing stupid things and getting hurt and people have to drive me to urgent care all the time and Wanda gets mad but not really mad, more worried, and I'm so embarrassed by how clumsy I am! I think this time Addie and Isa are going to fire me like they should have a long time ago!"

Amelia pats her back while my shoulders unbunch. This isn't a case of workplace violence, at least. "What caused this, Myra?"

She lowers her head. "I was in the refrigerator room, and I accidentally pulled a gallon of milk down on my face. Wanda's told me to use the stool a million times, but I was in a hurry. I was on my tiptoes, reaching up with my mouth open, and the stupid thing hit me right in the front teeth on the way down." She squints sadly. "Am I going to lose them? They feel like they might come out."

"I think they can be saved."

Myra wipes her teary eyes and crimson mouth and chin with a few tissues Amelia fetches her from the restroom, and then we escort her back to the kitchen where I tell Addie what I think. Wanda, standing at the worktable now, shakes her head again, but she does look relieved to hear Myra's teeth will probably be okay.

Addie takes Amelia and me aside and lowers her voice. "Here's the thing, and I know this isn't your problem at all, but we don't have a single extra driver to take her to the emergency dentist. I need every staff member I have tonight."

"Does she have any family in the area?" I ask.

Addie shakes her head. "Her husband Cory, Wanda's son, is a musician, and he's about to start a gig at a bar up in Breckenridge. We tried her sister, Madge, but no answer. I don't know what to do. I really need to get out and help Isa." She looks almost panicked.

I brace myself, not daring to look at Amelia. "I'll take her."

"No!" Addie and Amelia say it at the same time.

"You're needed here, too," Amelia says firmly. "I'll . . . ask Avery and Jason. They'll do it."

"I'd hate for them to miss the barbecue," I say.

"It's better than *you* missing the barbecue. It's for us, remember?"

She has a point.

"I'll call her right now." Amelia steps away, cell phone to her ear.

Addie wrings her hands. "I am so sorry about this, Travis. We've had staffing shortages before during the holidays, but this year is particularly bad."

"I get it. It's okay." I muster up a smile.

Addie and Isa have had a series of hiccups since they'd bought the ranch, and they'd confided in me that they almost lost it a couple of years in. But the last few years have been much better, especially after Tobias became the head wrangler, and the A-list actress, Kate Jordan, visited the ranch and gave a glowing review of her stay to her legion of fans. But staffing can be hard in remote areas, especially when the needs change dramatically between the popular summer and fall seasons and quieter winters and springs.

"Okay, they're coming," Amelia says. Her expression tells me she had to do some sweet talking with her sister. Avery can be hard-nosed, but she has a good heart.

"Thank you!" Addie hugs Amelia and me. "Now, you two get outside and enjoy your evening. We'll take care of Myra from here. Don't worry about a thing!"

Don't worry about a thing? We've been here a matter of hours and we've already had several near disasters.

What's next?

Chapter Six

THE CHRISTMAS SONG (CHESTNUTS ROASTING
ON AN OPEN FIRE)

Amelia

Travis and I walk out to the lobby where we're swept into a tinsel-y tangle of delighted greetings and bright smiles from guests we haven't seen yet. It's a blur of embraces, laughter, and brief catch ups. Through the mist of hugs and hellos, I spot Avery and Jason disappear into the kitchen to collect Myra. I hope she'll be okay.

Travis and I get separated in the crush of guests. There are enough people invited to fill the lodge's lobby, and the cheerful chatter dominates the space. While the crackling fire adds ambience to the room, I'm getting uncomfortably warm in my sweater and boots, and after a smothering bear hug by my great-uncle Norman, I smell like his spicy aftershave. I could use fresh air and food, which means that probably goes double for Travis.

Thankfully, after twenty minutes or so, Addie claps her hands to get the room's attention.

"Hello, everyone! I'm Addie Miller, one of the co-owners of

the Lazy Dog. I'd like to welcome you to the ranch and to Travis and Amelia's wedding weekend!"

Travis and I exchange smiles as everyone claps and cheers.

"I hope you all have had a chance to get a drink by now," Addie says, "and I know you're hungry for our chef Wanda's famous Rocky Mountain barbecue." A few people shout their approval, sounding like they're hungry *and* have had a couple of drinks already. "Great! So, let me tell you how we'll proceed."

She instructs us to form a line at the buffet tables to fill our plates and then to head outside to the patio where casual bar-type tables are set around the fire pit. On Addie's orders, Travis wades through our guests to my side and leads me to the head of the line.

I squeeze his forearm and lean close as we walk. "Ready for this?"

"Yes. For every bit of it." He gazes at me, his expression adoring. And then he grins. "Starting with some ribs."

We move along the banquet table filling our plates. We'd sampled everything a few months back while planning with Wanda and Addie, but seeing the dishes laid out, fresh and inviting, is heavenly. There are the ribs, pulled pork, roasted chicken, Wanda's secret recipe potato salad and dressed up macaroni and cheese, veggies, dips, and fruit, and an entire dessert table with several pies and cinnamon buns. I don't normally eat a lot of meat, but I try to get enough protein to last me through the night, knowing I'll be talking too much to eat the next few hours.

Plates in one hand, drinks in the other, Travis and I move outside to the carefully swept and salted patio. Addie, Isa, and Ruston have outdone themselves. Strings of white lights outline the wide pergola overhead, hurricane lanterns with tall, lit white candles are on every table, and tasteful holiday-themed arrangements circle the lanterns. The soft light glints off the snow surrounding the area, and a few ground-level landscaping lights, plus the cheerful fire in the pit in the center, creates the perfect winter vibe.

Standing close to Travis, grateful for my coat, boots, and the hat now, I eat as fast as I can without cramming it in before the first guests join us outside.

"Have you heard from Brent?" I ask between mouthwateringly smoky and savory bites. "Did he find Sev Two yet?"

He shakes his head. "Haven't heard from him. I thought I'd ask him when he gets here. He won't miss a chance to score free food."

"True." According to Sarah and Ben, Brent is a master at getting other people to pay for his meals, among other things. It's amazing everything we know about our clients, now that I think about it, from semi-regular check-ins with their pets. Sometimes I feel like we're therapists for our clients along with veterinary care providers.

Speaking of clients, a couple of them join us on the patio.

"Kathleen and Joe!" I set my still semi-full plate down to hug them.

Kathleen wears a light pink, thigh-length coat and a faux fur hat perched on top of her long, gorgeous strawberry-blond hair. Joe looks equally sharp, although he's wrapped so snugly in a coat, scarf, and hat that I can barely see his face. Although it's winter, and he moved to Colorado from Florida to be with Kathleen after they met at the CatFest Denver convention, he's still shockingly tan from years living on the Gulf Coast. I ask after Romeo and Juliet, their Instagram-famous Persian cat couple.

"They're in our cabin," Joe says. "We'd planned to leave them with James—"

"But he had a date!" Kathleen claps her hands excitedly.

My eyes widen with surprise. From their stories, Kathleen's brother James is kind of a nightmare. "With whom?"

She tells me about his new girlfriend, someone he met at work, while Joe and Travis catch up.

"James is still living in his own apartment, right?" I ask.

"For now. I think this woman might be the one for him, though," Kathleen says. "I hope so, anyway. He's matured a lot since Joe and I met. And I want him to be happy. And to stay independent."

I touch her hand. "I know you do. You've been incredibly supportive of him." Even when it had sometimes sounded like James didn't deserve it.

Her smile is grateful. "Thanks. I've tried my best."

Another set of guests wave at me as they come out to the patio.

"Oh!" I say. "There's another couple I'd love for you and Joe to meet. Beatrix! Can I introduce you and Seb to Kathleen and Joe? You're all huge cat lovers." I wink at Seb. He likes cats—he sort of has to being married to Beatrix and her many, many rescue cats—but he's maybe a touch less enthusiastic about felines than the other three.

As they greet each other and remind me that they'd all met briefly at one of the Love & Pets parties, an anxious look creeps across Bea's face. I step closer and lower my voice.

"Is everything okay? How's your dad?" Bea's father, a widower in Aspen, Colorado, is older, I know. And while she's told me things have improved, they've had a difficult relationship at times.

She brightens immediately. "He's fine. Everything's great!" Then her expression wobbles again behind her cat-eyed glasses. "But I'm worried about Fluff."

"What's wrong?"

I'm concerned but I keep my voice low. If Travis hears something's wrong with Fluffernutter, Bea's emotional support cat, he's going to feel compelled to offer to check her out. Promise or no promise to me, Fluff is like a part of Bea. She'd be lost without her. Travis turns slightly our way, although he still seems to be listening to Joe, Kathleen, and Seb's conversation.

"I don't want to bother you with it," Bea answers after a pause. "She'll be okay. And it's your wedding weekend! It's lovely so far, Amelia. The ranch was a perfect choice. Did I tell you that Seb and I brought Vilma, Robert, and a few other volunteers from the Colorado Cat Rescue up here for a weekend in the spring? We had such a great time."

"No, but that was wonderful of you! I'll bet they loved it." Although Bea is a successful romance writer, she's also independently wealthy thanks to a family inheritance.

She waves off my comment. "They deserved it. They worked so hard getting the new CCR facility built and running. And thank god it's done now; the planning almost killed me."

She rubs her eyes tiredly. Bea has unusually colored eyes: her right is hazel, and her left is blue. I've always loved her mismatched peepers, although I get the feeling she's sensitive about them. I hesitate, still not wanting Travis to overhear me, but I feel like I really should ask again.

"Are you sure you don't want to tell me about Fluff?"

She bites her lip. "Well—"

"Amelia. *Where* is your sister?" Mom interrupts from behind me.

I offer Bea an apologetic look and introduce them. My mother barely says hello before repeating her question. I excuse myself and take Mom aside to explain what happened.

She blinks. "Why did *they* have to take the woman? Doesn't the ranch have staff for this sort of thing?"

Of course, they should, but I don't want to throw Isa and Addie under the bus or incriminate Travis and myself any further for choosing the ranch as our venue. "They're unexpectedly shorthanded tonight."

Mom huffs out a breath that curls over her head in the cold air. "This is what you get when you have an event at a rustic ranch in the middle of nowhere."

"Mom, we're a little over an hour from Denver. Not exactly Antarctica."

"Don't sass me, Amelia. You know what I mean."

I take a deep breath. "Anyway, is there something I can do for you? Why did you need Avery?"

"Oh, nothing." She shakes her head, then seems to change her mind and tells me, "It's that woman." She's always referred to Suzanne as *that woman,* so I know immediately who she means. "She keeps staring at me."

"She's probably curious. When was the last time you saw each other?"

Mom tosses her hair back and thinks about it. The tips of her ears and fingers are bright red. She's not wearing a hat or gloves despite the near-freezing temperature. Too style conscious. "I suppose at your college graduation."

"That was forever ago. She hasn't seen you in a while."

"But must she stare?"

I glance in the direction of the fire pit where Mom shot a dark look. Suzanne *is* staring. At me, now, too. She doesn't look hostile, but then Suzanne has never been hostile to any of us. It's more . . . assessing. When she notices me looking, she turns back to my dad who's gazing pensively into the fire. Hmm.

"I don't know, Mom. Ignore her I guess."

"Do I have a choice?" she asks dramatically. "I don't want to make a scene at your wedding."

She could have fooled me. Time to change the subject. "Hey, have you met our friends Kathleen and Joe? They're Instagram influencers."

Mom knows exactly what an influencer is—someone somewhat famous—and I'm pretty sure it will impress her. She puts on her widest, glossiest smile as I make the introductions.

I stand beside Travis again, and our gazes connect. Everything okay? He asks with his eyes. I shrug, nod, and look around for my plate and drink, which I'd set down on the nearest table when I greeted Kathleen.

Although I'd only managed to take a few sips and scarf down a handful of bites, one of the wait staff had whisked it far away.

Ugh.

As I watch Bea frown and worry her bottom lip with her teeth, I consider telling Travis about Fluff, but . . . I don't. This is our wedding weekend, darn it, and I want to keep him to myself.

I'm not being *that* selfish.

Am I?

Chapter Seven

Travis

I knock on the door of the cabin and check my watch. Quarter to eleven. I have fifteen minutes at best.

A female voice answers. "Hold on a minute!"

I swipe the dusting of snowflakes off my shoulders and stamp my feet to clear my boots. The door opens and Bea peeks out, her glasses clouding in the chill air. She takes them off and peers at me.

"Travis! What are you—? Come in! Is everything okay?" A listless looking Fluff in her arms, Bea stammers as she scurries backward to open the door for me. Seb stands by the bathroom, pulling on a shirt.

"I know it's late," I say, "but I overheard you tell Amelia earlier that Fluff wasn't well. I wanted to check on her, if that's okay." I pick up my bag and step inside. "I only have a few minutes. I promised Amelia I wouldn't work this weekend, but she's at the lodge helping her mother with something, and our cabin is two doors down, so I thought I'd stop by."

Outside, the air outside is tinged with ice, but inside, it's toasty. Bea and Seb have their fireplace on.

She touches my arm. "That's so kind of you. But are you sure? You don't want to upset Amelia on the night before your wedding!"

"No kidding, brother, you don't," Seb jokes. He tilts his head at Bea. "This one would have killed me if I'd gone shooting after promising her I wouldn't during our wedding weekend."

Seb's a nature and wildlife photographer. Bea, one of my oldest clients, has complained before, mostly playfully, that her husband sneaks away to shoot every chance he gets. I don't think she really minds. As a professional author and genuine introvert, she needs plenty of time to herself, too.

"Yes, I would have." Bea gives him a look before turning back to me. "But . . . if you could take a super short peek at Fluff, I would be so grateful! If she needs anything, we can run her back to Boulder to the emergency vet and be back tomorrow in time for the wedding."

"Let's see what's going on." I glance around. "Can we put a towel or something on the bed, and I'll examine her there?"

Seb grabs the towel from the bathroom and Bea lays Fluff on it, then sits beside her. I pull out my stethoscope and a thermometer from the bag. The little tuxedo cat barely looks at me.

"Has there been a change in how much she's eating or drinking?" I ask.

Bea chews on her lip, thinking. "It's hard to tell, since all our cats share bowls, but I do think she's lost a little weight. She feels lighter to me."

"And she would know." Seb raises an eyebrow at me from where he's standing by the bed.

I smile, knowing he's right. Fluff is almost always either in Bea's arms or with her in her cat carrier. Bea watches me examine her cat, one hand on Fluff to comfort her and one slippered heel bouncing nervously on the ground. She glances anxiously from Fluff's face to mine.

"She does have a slight fever," I say after a few minutes, "and her abdomen seems tight and painful. Has she been vomiting or had diarrhea?"

Bea shrugs helplessly. "I'm not sure! I find it in the house sometimes but I'm never sure who does it!"

A consequence of having dozens of cats. "If I had to guess, I'd say it's a bacterial infection. It's hard to say what kind without more equipment, which means I'm not sure what would be best to prescribe. Amoxicillin and cephalexin are common, but there are others I'd prescribe if it's a urinary tract infection versus gastrointestinal. You could wait until Sunday to go to the emergency clinic, but—"

Bea shakes her head vehemently. "No. She's suffering, I can tell." She turns to her husband. "I'll drive her down. You stay here tonight and enjoy snowshoeing in the morning."

But he's already shaking *his* dark head. "No way, Bea. I'm not letting you drive her by yourself in the middle of the night in the snow. I'll go, too. Hopefully, we can come right back up in the morning with meds in hand." She smiles gratefully at him.

"If I had the RV here," I say, feeling helpless, "I could try to get a urine or fecal sample and take a look—"

Seb laughs. "Because looking at close-ups of cat pee and poop is every guy's fantasy for his wedding night."

"It's the night *before* the wedding," I joke. "So, you know, it would be fine."

"You've done more than enough already," Seb says. "We'll take care of Fluff from here."

"Yes, go back to your cabin and enjoy the rest of the evening," Bea says.

"I'll wash my hands first, if that's okay." I laugh and head for the bathroom. As I dry them, my phone rings. Addie's name appears on the screen. I answer. "Addie? Everything okay?"

"Bro," Brent says, "I found Sev Two. Can you come down to the place with the pool tables and stuff?"

At eleven at night? And why is Brent calling from Addie's phone? I sigh.

"Okay, Brent, but I don't have long." I can meet Amelia on her way back up to the Hitchin' Post. We'd agreed to share a glass of the champagne and a few chocolate-covered strawberries in our cabin to wrap up the day. A quiet drink together is something we haven't managed in weeks thanks to furious last-minute wedding preparations.

Bea grabs my coat to help me shrug into it while I talk. I switch the phone from one hand to another to get my gloves on. As I step outside, Bea thanks me in a whisper. I wave at her and Seb before hurrying across the Kissing Bridge to the activity center. The path is a bit slippery as the thin layer of snow turns to ice.

Lights are on inside the building. The kids, supervised by the ranch's resident kid wrangler, had a movie, games, and popcorn and stuff going earlier while the adults socialized, but that should be all wrapped up by now. My phone rings again—Amelia. Sorry Brent, I'm out of time. I stop to answer.

"Hey, love. Where are you? Everything okay with your mom?"

"I'm back at the cabin." She sounds exasperated and exhausted. "She couldn't find the diamond earrings she's planning to wear for the ceremony tomorrow. *Obviously,* an all-hands-on-deck emergency. Listen," she sighs, "I need your help . . . can you go back in time and arrange for me to be born to different parents?"

Chapter Eight
CHRISTMAS IN PRISON

Travis

I chuckle but sympathy floods my chest. "Maybe inviting her wasn't a great idea."

Some friends of ours walk by, laughing and talking. They wave with surprised expressions when they see me. I wave back cheerfully, trying to give the impression that it's perfectly normal for the groom to be outside alone and on the phone in the freezing cold, the night before his wedding.

"No, you were right to encourage me to invite her. She's driving me crazy, but I'd probably regret it later if she wasn't here. And Dad, too." Amelia yawns. "Where are you?"

"Brent called. He said he found Sev Two and needs my help. I can tell him I can't . . . but I thought if we can corral Sev tonight that might be for the best."

"Yes, absolutely. Go help Brent. I ran into Sarah and Ben in the lobby as I left. They helped look for him too, but no luck. I'll get ready for bed, read my book, and wait for you to get back for our drink."

"I'll make it quick, then. Have you heard from Avery?" I've been thinking about them. Mountain roads can be dangerous at night.

"They're still at the dentist's office with Myra. They're wrapping up, though. Her teeth can be saved, thank goodness. They'll bring her home and be back soon, Avery said."

"Glad it wasn't worse. Hey, Amelia?"

"Yes?"

"Tomorrow can't get here soon enough."

I pocket my phone, open the door, and walk inside the activity center. The place is still and quiet. An open area in the middle holds table games like foosball, air hockey, ping pong, and two pool tables, some small bar tables and a snack center with things like a coffee machine, fridge, popcorn machine, and a snack counter that the staff mans during the day. A few other rooms are accessible from here, including a small movie theater and the kids club where parents can drop their children for some fun during the day while they relax.

I stop a few feet inside and call for Brent. He better not have asked me to meet him and then ditched me. It didn't take me *that* long to get here. On the other hand, if he did, then I can join Amelia sooner for that drink.

"Back here!"

Brent's muffled voice comes from somewhere in the back. Switching on lights as I go, I follow the echo of his voice through an open doorway into a room set up with several rows of shabby chairs. On the wall, a white board lists staff member names and whether they're working this weekend or not. A second board lays out the timeline for our wedding activities from the barbecue reception tonight straight through to brunch on Sunday morning before everyone heads home.

"Brent?" I call again.

"Keep going." His voice comes from metal double doors across the room. "But when you open the doors, close them quick."

It's warm now that I'm inside, so I take off my coat, hang it on a chair, and drop my gloves with it. Then, in one swift motion, I open the doors and scuttle inside. They shut behind me with a jarring metallic scrape.

The room is bright, too bright, thanks to fluorescent lighting overhead, and the space smells like laundry detergent. Industrial-sized washing machines and dryers line the walls, and carts of laundry sit around with sizable mountains of dirty towels and sheets in some and clean and folded piles in others. A desk sits against one wall, and shelves with boxes of cleaning supplies line another. Counter space is in limited supply, currently covered with unopened packages of toilet paper, tissue boxes, and other stuff housekeepers need.

I glance around, finally locating Brent halfway inside one of the dryers.

"Sev's not in there, is he?" I ask.

"Nope. But he's here somewhere." Brent's voice echoes inside the machine. He pulls his head out and sticks it in the next dryer. "He'd probably like the dryers because they might still be warm. Can you look around for him, too?"

"I thought you said you knew he was here." I lean over the nearest laundry cart, moving the linens around carefully.

"I already looked there, bro. Try the desk."

"Would he be in the desk for any particular reason?" I ask.

"No. But I haven't looked there."

Head shaking, I open drawers and sift papers around. Sev Two is big enough that a cursory glance is good enough to rule out most places. Brent's right, though; he'll hide somewhere in or under or behind things, and warm places would be especially tempting to him.

"So . . . why do you think he's in here again?" I drop to all fours to check under and behind the desk and nearby shelving.

"Welp, Sarah and Ben and me looked all over the lodge for him, and no dice. So, after you saw his poo in the laundry place on my floor in the lodge, those women that run this place suggested I look here, because this is where the housekeepers bring the dirty stuff from rooms. The blonde one let me in and let me use her phone to call you."

"Where's your phone?" I ask.

"Dead."

I move on to checking some boxes of detergent piled on the floor. "And you're sure he's not in your room?"

"No, but I looked all over there first and didn't see him."

Which means he's still not at all certain where Sev Two is, is what I'm gathering. Which means we might be completely wasting our time. But whatever. A few more minutes won't hurt.

As I search, I alternate between checking my watch and dusting my pants off after being on my hands and knees. Brent's still in the jeans and hoodie he'd worn before the barbecue. And now that I think about it—

"Were you at the barbecue?" I ask.

"Naw, I was looking for Sev Two." He sits, his hands on his knees and his back against the doors to the staff room outside. "Glad to know I was missed."

"Sorry, buddy, there were a lot of people there. I didn't get to talk to some of my own family." What's left of it. I only have an aunt, uncle, and a trio of cousins here. After Jo died, we hadn't been good at keeping in touch. Which is also why I think it's important for Amelia's family to be here.

Brent grins. "I'm messing with you, bro." He goes back to looking, and that's when the truth hits me: Sev Two is Brent's family.

He might be a fifty-pound boa constrictor, but the death of Sev One sent Brent into a pet grief support group. Sev Two means as much to him, if not more. Family is family.

What if Doug, Daisy, or the Four Horsemen of the Apocalypse, the band of scruffy dogs that I've had since before Amelia and I met, went missing? Or Charlie, my bison? I'd be as worried as Brent, and I'd hope a friend would help me find them. I can spare another ten minutes of searching. Amelia will probably be asleep by now anyway.

But after ten minutes, there's no sign of Sev. No snake feces either.

"I don't know, Brent, maybe we should call it a night. I can let Addie and Isa know that he's still on the loose, and they can ask the housekeepers to watch out for him tomorrow while they clean the ranch." I'm sure that will be popular news among the housekeeping staff.

Brent stands and stretches. He shrugs, trying to look okay with it, but his expression is pinched, and the normally dark half-moons under his eyes are even darker. I clap him on the shoulder as we walk to the door.

"I can't promise I'll have time to look for him tomorrow, but we'll look all day Sunday if he doesn't turn up."

Brent smirks at me. "What about your honeymoon?"

I grin back. "We don't leave until Tuesday."

"Where are you taking her?"

"Costa Rica for some beach time, rainforest time, and . . . they have this giant dog rescue there where the dogs run free, and you can go and hang out with them. It's called Territorio de Zaguates. It means Land of Strays—"

My voice trails off. Brent's been trying to pull open the double doors, but they won't budge. He yanks again. Nothing. And there are no outside doors to this room. This is the lone exit.

"Let's try it together." We both pull the door handles. Again, there's barely a shiver.

I let out a long, frustrated breath. "I'll call someone to let us out."

I won't bother Amelia, and I hate to call Isa, Tobias, or Addie so late, but they'd also have the key in case it had somehow locked from the outside when I came in—

I pat my back pocket and let loose a curse. My cell phone's in the pocket of my coat. Which is outside. Hanging neatly on the back of the chair.

A prickly feeling crawls across my back as my eyes shoot to the desk. No wired telephone. The housekeepers all carry walkie talkies, I remember.

Tugging on the door more does nothing. It might as well be laughing in our faces.

My thoughts spin. Amelia will wake up in the morning, find me missing, and freak out. I wince, imagining her panic.

I shove my fingers into my hair and think if there's anything else we can do to get out of here. But we've already searched the room, and nothing comes to mind. Crap, crap, crap.

Brent saunters over to a laundry cart, one with a soft pile of towels, and rolls himself over the edge and inside.

"What are you doing?" I ask.

He looks at me like I'm stupid. "Getting some sleep. Hit the light, will you?"

That confirms it. I'm spending the night before my wedding in the ranch's laundry land with Brent. And, possibly, a massive adolescent boa constrictor.

This weekend is getting better by the minute.

Chapter Nine

WHERE ARE YOU CHRISTMAS?

Amelia

The morning of our wedding day, bright sunlight streams through the cracks around the heavy drapes covering the wide cabin windows. I pry open my eyes, stretch my neck and shoulders, and say a sleepy good morning to Travis. He doesn't answer, so I turn his way, ready to burrow into his warmth.

Dougie's flat and wrinkled face is an inch from mine. He grins and offers me a sloppy kiss. Daisy whines. I sit up, wiping my face with the back of my hand.

"Travis?" The bathroom door is open. No lights or sounds from there. In fact, the cabin looks exactly like I left it when I went to bed. The dregs of a cold cup of tea lurks on the nightstand and my book sprawls on the floor, where it probably dropped after I fell asleep last night.

There are no signs of Travis's shed clothing from last night, and now that I think about it, I don't remember him letting himself in. I wasn't *that* tired.

"Where is he?" I mutter to the dogs as I crawl out of the

warm king size bed. I'd slept well. Too well, apparently. Worry scratches at my nerves. I check the time—six o'clock—and grab my phone to check if he'd called or texted. Nothing since I spoke to him last night. And I can't find his phone on Find My Friends.

I call Avery. It's early, but she'll understand. My sister sounds like a sleepy frog when she answers.

"Aves, hey. Did Myra get home okay?" I ask in a rush.

"Mm, yeah. We dropped her off and got back here around midnight." Her voice clears a little. "I know you're excited to get married and everything, but it's sorta early. You okay?"

"Um, not really. Travis is missing."

"What?" She suddenly sounds as sharp as a syringe needle. "Since when?"

"I don't know. I woke up, and he wasn't here. I don't think he came in last night." I tell her about our call last night. "He might be with Brent, but why wouldn't he text or something to let me know where he was going? Should I call the police?"

"Whoa, hang on. Let's start with checking around here," Avery says. "Are you dressed?"

"No, I just woke up, and the pugs need to eat and go out, and . . . I need to pee."

"Okay. Here's the plan: pee, get dressed, and call Addie and Isa and get them to ask the staff to help look for Travis. Jason and I will be right over. He can take care of the dogs while we search."

"Got it. Thank you, Avery." I love my sister. She can be overbearing at times, but at other times, like this time, she's a take charge kind of girl. Unlike, well, me.

With fear tangling my insides, I use the restroom, put on a coat and boots over my pajamas, and call Isa. If she's with Tobias, like she probably would be this early, then I get two people looking for Travis for the time spent on one phone call. She answers, sounding fully awake, thank goodness.

"Isa—Travis didn't come home last night."

"Really?" In the background, I hear a distinctly male rumble, so Tobias must still be there. I fill her in on what I know, which isn't much, and she relays the information to her husband. "I'll check with Addie, housekeeping, and the kitchen staff right away. They all should get to work any time now. Tobias will check the lodge and activity center on the way to the barn and stables. Try not to worry, Amelia. If he's here, we'll find him within minutes."

Someone knocks on the door, and the pugs bark like it's the second coming of Satan. I peek out the window. "Avery and Jason are here," I tell Isa. "Please let me know what you find out. Oh, and Myra is going to be okay."

"I heard. Thank them again for taking her to the emergency dentist. We owe you all one."

I want to say something nice, like we're a wedding team, but I'm too upset. When I answer the door, Jason looks tired, cold, and grumpy, but he greets Daisy and Doug with the high-pitched voice that never fails to work them into a frenzy. Between the barking, whining, and Jason's voice, I'm grateful that this cabin doesn't share walls with any other rooms.

As I pull on a hat and gloves, I give Jason hurried instructions on where the leashes are, where the dog food is, and who eats what. Daisy gets a special dog food for allergies and is taking an antibiotic right now for a urinary tract infection, so she has a probiotic, too, to help with stomach upset from the medication.

Then Avery and I rush out the door, only to realize we have no idea which direction to go. Luckily, we spot Tobias heading down to the activity center. We call to him and catch up at the Kissing Bridge.

The tall, lean head wrangler tips his ever-present cowboy hat at us. He's also wearing his usual jeans, boots, and a heavy winter work coat. I've never seen Tobias out of his cowboy garb.

"I'm checking out the activity center. Want to join me?" he asks.

"Yes, please. Thanks for looking for Travis, Tobias. I have no idea where my fiancé could have gotten to . . . overnight." The last word peters out as a horrible thought hits me.

It's the morning of our wedding. Should I have checked for Travis' suitcase in our room? Or checked the parking lot for a missing car? Could he have had last minute second thoughts and bailed on our wedding weekend and on . . . me?

Avery glances at me as if she can read my mind. "He's here. He must have gotten into a scrape of some kind. Probably because of an animal." Her face pinches.

"Sounds like the doc," Tobias says easily.

I nod. It does. I trust Travis Brewer with all of my heart. He would never be a runaway groom. If he had second thoughts, he'd talk to me about them. He'd never be so cruel as to wait until our wedding weekend to call off our engagement.

I think.

Tobias opens the door to the center. A single light is on inside. No sign of any guests. There will be soon, I'll bet. It's almost six-thirty now. Plenty of people are early risers, even on vacation, and even when the temperature outside hovers right above freezing. Our guests will be looking for coffee and break-fast soon, and we should be with them.

"Doc?" Tobias calls. We stop to listen for a response. Nothing.

We search around the different parts of the center. I check the movie theater, imagining Travis falling asleep in one of those comfortable theater chairs . . . for some reason. Avery walks through the Little Wranglers Room and comes out shaking her head. Tobias moves toward the back of the center. We follow him.

He throws on the lights in a dimly-lit room with a few rows of chairs and a couple of whiteboards. A woman stands by a set of metal double doors. As the lights come on, she shrieks.

The surprise of the woman and her scream make Avery and me jump and Tobias stiffen. His shoulders relax a moment later.

"Damn, Teresa, you scared the horseflies off me."

The tiny Latina woman standing by the doors heaves a deep breath in and says, "You did too, boss."

He pushes his hat back off his forehead. "Sorry about that. Everything okay?"

"My key won't fit in the lock, and I can't get the doors to open."

"Well, let me help." Tobias introduces us quickly to Teresa, the head housekeeper at the ranch, and then tries her key in the lock. It clearly won't turn. He pulls hard on the door. A moment later, there's a heavy pounding from the other side.

This time, Teresa, Avery, and I *all* scream.

"Get us out of here!" A man yells from behind the doors. A man that sounds a lot like—

"Brent? Is that you?" I move closer.

"Yeah. Hey, Amelia."

My heart gallops with hope. "Is Travis with you?"

A second, exhausted-sounding voice answers. "I'm here."

I put a hand flat on the door, imagining Travis's hand on the other side, my heart pounding with relief. "What are you two doing in there?"

"We got stuck last night. The doors wouldn't open."

Teresa nods, like she told us so.

"Why didn't you call or text me?" I ask.

"My coat and cell phone are out there, and Brent's is charging in his room," is the reply from inside.

Sure enough, Travis's coat hangs on a chair.

"Hang on, fellas, we'll get you out," Tobias said.

"Morning, Tobias," Travis says. "Thanks."

"Hey brother-in-law," Avery says with a wry smile at the door. "Sleep well?"

"You here too, Avery? Not especially. Turns out a laundry cart isn't a super comfortable bed."

"Imagine that," my sister says.

"Can you call Isabel and let her know we found them?" Tobias asks.

I give Avery my phone to call Isa, grateful again that my sister is here by my side. I join Tobias by the door. After a few more strong yanks on the handle, he shines his phone flashlight at the lock.

"Looks like a key broke off in the lock."

"That would be Dale," Teresa says, crossing her arms. She still has her winter gear on, and a large tote bag over her shoulder. "It happened before, and Phil fixed it."

"Okay—Phil will be in at noon," Tobias says.

My eyes bulge. "Noon?" I vaguely remember meeting Phil, the ranch's handyman, during one of our visits.

"Hopefully we don't have to wait on him." Tobias rummages around in a cabinet on the wall and pulls out a hammer. "I'll have to try to take the door off the hinges. We don't want these two to starve to death inside. And even worse, if our guests don't get clean towels and an empty wastepaper basket, right, T?" He winks at Teresa. She laughs and agrees with a knowing look.

I chuckle, too. I could laugh all day now that I know Travis is okay. And that he still wants to marry me.

"All right, you boys stand back," Tobias says to the door. Then, he mutters, "Wish I had a screwdriver."

Teresa eyes him as he aims at the hinge. "You don't want to hit it too hard—"

A moment later, he drives the hammer up—hard—against one of the hinges. Then he hits it again.

"Well this is embarrassing," Tobias says, examining his work. "I bent it." Teresa rolls her eyes and takes a seat in one of the chairs. Avery and I exchange glances. Looks like this might take a while.

"Amelia?" Travis says.

"Yes?" I answer.

"Why don't you go back to the room. As soon as we get out, I'll join you."

I glance at Avery and she nods with wide eyes. Yes, please,

she's saying. I hate to leave my fiancé stuck here, but on the other hand, there isn't much we can do to help.

"Okay. See you soon," I say to the door. "I love you."

"I love you, too. I'm sorry about this."

"Me, too."

I touch Tobias' shoulder and thank him for helping. He apologizes again as he examines the warped hinge. And then I thank Teresa for doing the hard work of cleaning up after us and our guests.

As Avery and I leave the center, a few people already wander down toward the lodge where breakfast should be served soon. Everyone's free to enjoy the ranch activities this morning before lunch, and then, barring any more emergencies, sleigh rides are scheduled in the afternoon.

"I was hoping for a little more sleep, but I guess we at least have time to shower now." And I might actually relax and enjoy it, now that I know Travis is safe.

Avery's phone rings. "Jay? We're on—"

Through the speaker, I can hear her boyfriend's voice, more urgent than normal, along with the unmistakable, pitiful sounds of a pug retching.

Chapter Ten
BLUE CHRISTMAS

Amelia

"What happened? Is he . . . okay?" I pant as I run up the hill to the Hitchin' Post. Avery's hot on my heels after thrusting her phone at me to talk to Jason.

"I don't know," he sounds stressed out. "I took them out, fed them, and we hung on the couch for a while, and then he started puking."

"In the cabin?"

"Yeah. Kind of all over."

I groan. "Almost . . . there."

Jason has the door open by the time Avery and I make it to the porch. My breath steams in the cold air and I'm sweating now, too. Doug and Daisy are attached to their leashes and on the porch, where Doug continues to retch. I kneel beside him, keeping a careful distance. Daisy seems normal as far as I can tell.

"Dougie, are you okay?"

He responds with a loud belch and a mournful look. Seriously, there's no look more mournful than a pug's mournful look.

"How many times has he vomited?" I ask Jason while petting my dog gingerly.

"I'm not sure. It was like one extended spew session," he says.

Since Doug seems okay for the moment, I step inside to see how bad it is. My nose wrinkles, and I grimace as I view the damage. Chunks of food sit in small pools of yellow bile all over the room. Yeah, pretty bad.

I examine the food bowls. Daisy's is empty and licked clean. Doug's bowl has some food left inside and a small trail of kibble leading away from the bowl. I step back outside.

"I think I know what happened. Doug ate Daisy's food—medication, probiotics, and all—and Daisy ate Doug's."

Daisy always makes a mess and leaves some food when she eats. Doug is a neat eater, and never leaves a single bite leftover. Given the state of their respective bowls, I'm almost positive I'm right.

"No, they didn't," Jason says, "I saw them eat their own . . . oh, wait. I guess they could have. Damn, I'm sorry Amelia."

"Doug should be okay now that Daisy's food and medication are out of his stomach."

I'd feel better if Travis had an operational cell phone so I could consult with him about it. I could go back down to the activity center, but I decide to trust my own gut—so long as Doug doesn't vomit again.

"Well," Avery sighs, "let's get the dog puke cleaned up."

In the bright morning sun, my sister and her boyfriend look exhausted. Avery's eyes are puffy, and her face is pale. Jason's shoulders slump over his lanky frame, and he looks like he could really use a shower.

I shake my head. "You two have done so much already—taking Myra to the hospital, waking up at the crack of dawn to help me—and you haven't had a minute to relax and enjoy the weekend. I've got this; you go back to your cabin."

They glance at each other.

"No," Avery says. "We don't mind helping."

"Mom will probably be calling you any minute about some emergency or another. I spent half an hour last night helping her find a pair of earrings that were right there in her jewelry bag." I take the dogs' leashes from them. "Go. Relax. Have fun. Thank you so much for all of your help."

Avery looks torn, but Jason tugs on her arm, and finally they step off the porch, heading back toward their own cabin.

"Sorry again about Doug," Jason says as they go.

"And I hope Travis breaks out soon," Avery adds.

"Breaks out?" Jason asks her. "Was he arrested last night?"

I sigh and lead the dogs in to put them in their crate. They should stay contained until I know if Doug's stomach has settled. As it is, we'll have to pay to clean the cabin's pretty Navajo-style rug that Doug did his best to ruin.

I'll mop up the mess, keep an eye on Doug, and get myself ready for some cross-country skiing, the activity Travis and I chose for the morning. It will be wonderful to skim along together on the packed snow getting fresh air and exercise under the bluebird Colorado sky. Assuming Doug is okay by then and Travis, er, breaks out.

But before all of that . . . coffee.

I put a pod into the coffee machine in our kitchenette and retrieve a mug from the shelf above, then root around for some sugar and creamer in the little basket beside the machine. This is the first moment I've had to myself since we arrived at the Lazy Dog yesterday. And it will probably be the *single solitary* moment I have to myself, given that it's our wedding day.

Our wedding day.

I can't believe it's finally here. I keep saying that, but it's because I've waited *so* long for this. From the painful saga with my old boyfriend Tim, with whom I share dog-custody of Doug and who was the first person I *thought* I'd marry, to meeting Travis, dating, adopting Daisy together, entering school to become a veterinary technician, joining Travis in his Love & Pets mobile practice, and finally getting engaged.

Our wedding day has been a long time coming. Now, if only I had my groom.

After a couple of sips of the overly sweet beverage, I crack open the windows and get to work. An hour later, the room is clean, fresher smelling, and *I'm* clean and fresher smelling. I'm gathering my cross-country gear out of the closet—leggings, long-sleeve workout shirt, and a fleece—when there's a tap on the door.

"Hang on!" I yell and tie my hotel robe sash tighter around my waist. I love these luxurious robes so much; I should buy one. Isa and Addie sell them and other branded things in the little hotel kiosk by the front desk.

I open the cabin door, and find, speak of the devil, Isa and Addie, and their three adorable dachshunds Zip, Zap, and Zoom on the porch. The dogs go berserk when they see me— barking, jumping up and down, and gnawing on their own and each other's leashes—which makes Doug and Daisy go equally nuts in their crate.

I greet the dogs and reluctantly let them all in rather than making them stand on the porch with me in my robe. I hope I did a good enough job cleaning.

"Sorry to interrupt, Amelia," Isa says, "but we wanted to let you know that we haven't been able to get the laundry area doors open. Tobias tried removing them from their hinges and then taking the lock and door handle apart, but, well—" She glances at Addie with a pained look.

"His strengths lie in equine management, not in handyman jobs," Addie finishes diplomatically. "I called our maintenance technician, Phil, and we tried five different locksmiths, but no one can get here until noon. Which means—"

"Travis is stuck in there until lunchtime," I finish dejectedly.

Addie rushes forward to take my hand. "We know you and Travis had plans this morning, and of course we feel terrible that he spent the night in the housekeeping area instead of the cabin you paid for. We'll be offering you a deep discount on the weekend, and we'll do anything we can do to make this up to you."

As the three Z's strain on their leashes to sniff at the rolled up, soiled rug in the corner, I tell them it's okay. Of course, I wish it hadn't happened, but it doesn't seem like they could have prevented it, and I know they're doing everything they can to make it right. I can carry on by myself this morning and enjoy spending time with our guests. And without Travis.

"Do they have food and water?" I'm sorry to say I hadn't thought about it before.

"They have bottles of water, and we told them to eat anything in the housekeepers mini-fridge." Addie looks ashamed. "They've shared a leftover sandwich, a packaged salad, and a slice of cheesecake that they split between them. We have one of the housekeepers posted by the door in case there's an emergency . . . beyond being locked up, I mean."

I smile sadly. "Will you keep me posted on how they are? I'll have my phone with me."

"Of course." Addie squeezes my hand. "And we promise to make tonight the most amazing wedding you'll ever have!" She pauses. "Not that you'll have another wedding . . ." Isa shakes her head.

I put on a brave face for them as they apologize for the fifth time and leave. This afternoon, once Travis is freed from the housekeeping jail, everything will be perfect. It has to be.

Because everything *before* noon has pretty much been a disaster.

Chapter Eleven
LONELY THIS CHRISTMAS

Travis

"What do you think they're doing out there?" Brent asks.

I sigh. "Sleeping in. Hiking. Snowshoeing. Hanging out by the fire. Eating breakfast."

He groans. "Don't talk about food, bro. I'm starving." His stomach growls as if to emphasize his statement. The leftovers from the housekeeping fridge didn't go too far.

At least we have a bathroom. The last twelve hours would have been catastrophic without it.

I check my watch—11:30 am—and resume pacing around the room. I'm trying to get to ten-thousand steps before we get sprung. I'm at nine thousand. It's surprisingly hard to put one foot in front of the other one thousand times when you're watching the number tick up so slowly.

Aside from needing to move after a stiff and uncomfortable night folded into a laundry cart, I'm worried about what Amelia will say when I finally get out of here. After all, if I hadn't reneged on my promise and offered to help Brent, I wouldn't be in this mess. I'd promised I wouldn't, but I hadn't been able to help myself. If Sev Two had been in here, it would have justified breaking my promise. But he clearly is not.

And, if I'm being honest, I'm also really tired of being in the same small room with Brent. He isn't the chattiest of guys at the best of times, and . . . well, this isn't the best of times. Right now, he's lying on his back on the desk, his boots resting against the shelf on one side, humming off tune. Without our cell phones, a book, a bottle of tequila, *something*, it's damn hard to pass the time.

I hear voices from outside and rush over. I yell to Dale, the housekeeping sentry who's posted outside. "Is it the locksmith?"

"Yes sir," Dale says in his thick Southern accent.

He's been a nice guy, very sympathetic, all morning. We'd heard him chortling while watching YouTube videos outside. There isn't much he can do for us but knowing someone was there if we'd needed them had helped.

Brent rolls off the desk and almost falls on his face. He bangs on the door. "Get us out of here, bro!"

I throw him an exasperated look. "Give the guy a minute."

Someone laughs. "Keep your pants on, cherry pie."

Whoops. Hello, stupid assumptions. The voice that answers is female. And sounds like it belongs to a 65-year-old pack-a-day smoker. I couldn't care less so long as she has the skills and tools to get these doors open. Brent and I hover while she does something that sounds like the equivalent of taking apart a car engine with a blow torch.

In less than two minutes, she yells, "Stand back, apple fritters!"

These apple fritters do, and shortly after the entire lock and handle mechanism is yanked out of one of the doors, and then the other. The doors magically open.

The locksmith stands with her hands on her wide hips and a grin on her lined face. Her hair is a mass of unruly brown and gray curls, and she wears one of those old school gray jumpsuits.

"Good morning, frosted brownies. You two look a little overbaked."

Dale, a skinny man with thinning brown hair who looks to be about forty, laughs. "It's more like afternoon, Willa."

"I don't think these bear claws care what time it is so long as they get out of here. Do you, bear claws?"

Brent and I shake our heads. "No, ma'am."

I pump Willa and Dale's hands on the way by. "Thank you very much for your help, but I've got a wedding weekend to get back to! See you later, Brent."

I grab my coat and gloves, which are still on the chair, check for my phone—two percent power left—and sling the coat on as I rush through the bustling activity center. Some of Amelia and my neighbors and a few friends hang around the tables, playing ping pong and air hockey with their kids, but I don't slow down.

This weekend was meant to be fun for everyone, but for me, it's all about Amelia. I need to get back by her side, and I don't plan to leave it until we are man and wife. Or wife and man. Any which way is fine by me.

But as I bust through the outer doors, I almost trip over a trio of small mammals. The resident dachshunds Zip, Zap, Zoom are right outside attached to leashes held by Addie. They bark and jump up and down on my leg, which I can't resist. I kneel down to pet them. They're wearing green and red bows tied to their collars.

Through the long night of the soul in Laundryland Prison, I'd almost forgotten it was practically Christmas, along with our wedding day. Ho, ho, ho.

"You're out!" Addie says triumphantly.

"Yes, the locksmith worked quick." Once she actually got here. "Have you seen Amelia?"

"She was cross-country skiing with some folks the last time I saw her. And having a great time, I promise."

That makes me happy to hear. And a little sad to have missed out. But mostly happy.

Addie goes on, "But it's almost lunchtime. She might be back at your cabin getting ready?"

I rush off, the Z's barking excitedly at my sudden departure. I walk up the hill, texting Amelia that I'm free and headed to the Hitchin' Post, right as my phone dies. No big deal, I'm almost there. As I turn to take the path to our cabin, the door of the place nearest to ours opens and our clients Kathleen and Joe step out.

"Look—it's the star of the show!" Joe hops off the porch to shake my hand.

I curse under my breath. They don't know I've been locked up all night, so I can't exactly run by them without stopping to at least say hello.

Despite what's really a pretty warm day for December in the mountains, Joe wears a hat, car coat, gloves, knee-high snow boots, and a thick scarf that he has to yank his chin out of to speak. I guess you can take the man out of Florida, but you can't take Florida completely out of the man. Not that I'd want to. Joe's a good guy.

"We hoped we'd catch you alone for a moment," Kathleen says, following him to stand beside me. Her golden red hair falls almost to her waist over her pink coat. "We have a little wedding gift for you and Amelia, but it takes a bit of explaining."

"I have to . . . I mean, I've been . . ." I sigh. How can I say no? "Of course I have a few minutes for our favorite clients from Colorado Springs."

Kathleen swats my arm. "We're your only clients from Colorado Springs, aren't we?"

"Nope," I lie as I follow them back inside their cabin. Even if Amelia and I had other clients in the Springs, Kathleen and Joe would probably still be our favorites.

Their cabin is arranged a lot like the Hitchin' Post with the king-sized bed, kitchenette, and fireplace, but it's maybe a little smaller and less luxurious. After a glance around, I find Juliet and

Romeo, Kathleen and Joe's famous Shakespearean cats, lounging in front of the fireplace.

"Hey there, you two. How goeth things?" I ask the Persians, one a silver chinchilla female with white fur and green eyes, and the other a handsome black male with amber eyes. As I reach out to pet them, Juliet curls up against my left hand and purrs . . . which seems to make Romeo jealous.

The black cat bats my hand away, scratching my hand and slicing—what else? —my bare ring finger. A line of blood wells up from the long but shallow wound.

"Romeo!" Joe scoops up his cat and pops him into an open crate beside the door. "Bad cat!"

"Are you all right?" Kathleen asks me, her forehead wrinkling with concern. "Let me clean that and get you a Band-Aid. I have one in my purse." She rushes around, but I shake my head.

"Do you have a tissue? I've got to get back to our cabin and take a shower before lunch anyway."

The scratch burns, but cleaning and dressing it will take more time. After some fussing, Kathleen hands me the tissue, which I wrap tightly around my finger. Then, finally, she retrieves a small cream-colored gift bag from on top of the dresser.

"I wish Amelia were here, too, but you can explain it to her when she re-opens it later."

The mention of my fiancée makes me squirm. I should probably already be down at the lodge for lunch. But I screw on a polite smile and wait for Kathleen to present the gift. She hands it to me.

"Of course, you know that Joe and I met at CatFest in Denver, and that's how we ended up forming our company, Catcall. Our partnership has led to the cats and us," she smiles at Joe, "to be asked to several conventions as invited guests, and it's always an amazing time. Since we know you and Amelia are cat lovers too, next year, we'd love to have you join us." She nods at the bag, which I open.

Two glittery tickets to CatFest NYC are inside, along with vouchers for flights from Denver.

"You guys, this is incredible! But you're too generous. This is way too much—"

Joe shakes his head. "You both were there when we met, and you've been incredible with Romeo and Juliet even when one of them doesn't deserve it." He glares at the cat carrier. "We think we'd all have a great time together, so we hope you'll come. We'll get your hotel room, too, by the way."

"This is fantastic. Thank you." It really is a generous gift, and for animal lovers like Amelia and me it would be a blast, not to mention an opportunity to learn and network. I'm touched, and I have a feeling Amelia might burst into tears when she opens the gift. We haven't had much time or opportunity to travel since we met.

After catching up with Kathleen and Joe for a few more minutes, I hustle back to our cabin and throw the door open, more than ready to put my arms around Amelia and tell her about the gift. My finger still stings and throbs, and I smell like a mixture of sweat and commercial laundry detergent, but I'm planning to not let her go until we have to go to lunch.

Except . . . she's not here.

Doug and Daisy are in their crate, and Doug seems less excited to see me than usual. Otherwise the room is empty. As I let them out to play, I plug my phone in to charge and wait impatiently for it to start back up. My heart sinks when I get Amelia's text. She's already down at the lodge.

Miss you, babe, her text says.

Yeah, I think. I miss you, too.

Chapter Twelve
THINKING ABOUT DRINKING FOR CHRISTMAS

Amelia

"Where is Travis?" Mom asks me—again. "He hasn't left you at the altar, has he?"

I wince as she titters. Avery scowls behind Mom's back; it's threatening to become a permanent expression.

We're sitting at the designated family table in the lodge and lunch is about to be served. The room looks about the same as last night, except that instead of a buffet table, we're all seated at round tables, like we will be tonight. Ruston put a few of the arrangements from last night out as centerpieces, but he'd told me earlier that he would save the best displays for tonight.

I look over at Ruston and Kenny and catch them whispering and glancing at the empty seat next to me. I groan to myself. As little as Travis and I have been together for the last twenty hours or so, I'm not surprised that people are wondering what's going on.

I haven't told anyone that Travis and Brent got stuck in the housekeeping area. First, it's hard to explain why they were in there without mentioning the search for Severus the Second. And I don't want our guests to panic any more than they already have about the missing boa constrictor.

Second, I don't want the consequences of the damaged doors to reflect badly on Isa and Addie. A few things were bound to go wrong this weekend. Of course, I thought it might be something minor like a room mix-up, a small shortage of wine, or maybe delayed flights or a traffic jam making our guests late. I wasn't expecting the groom to be trapped overnight and have to sleep in a laundry cart, but here it is.

And third, I don't want to talk about it. I'm stressed about what else might go wrong today, and . . . I'm nervous about getting married.

Yes, I'm as excited as a bride can be. But it's the first, and I hope the only, time I'll dedicate my life to someone, while they dedicate their life to me. It's scary. And my mom, and even sometimes Avery, aren't helping.

Mom's been dropping not-so-subtle reminders of all the people in our lives who've divorced. There was my aunt Lisa, my uncle Charles on the other side, my mom's best friend Becky, Avery's coworkers Jim and his wife, and Becca and her wife, my mother's neighbors on *both* sides . . . and the list goes on.

But chief among them are Mom and Dad themselves. Growing up, I didn't have a great example when it came to marriage, the divorce was downright awful, and my mother won't let me forget it. My dad might as well be the devil, as far as she's concerned.

Huh. Speak of the devil, here he is.

Dad and Suzanne sit down beside me at the table and directly across from Mom. Avery and I lock eyes. It would be better if the positioning was a little less . . . confrontational . . . but it's too late now.

I cast a desperate glance at the door, looking for Travis. Still no sign of him. Not that he can do anything to help. Everything's just easier with him by my side.

"Hi, Dad, Suzanne," I say brightly. "Did you have a good morning? I didn't see you at breakfast or out on the trails."

Dad glances at his wife and puts his hand on hers. Mom's expression is as sour as cranberries. "No, we slept in. The altitude makes it difficult to get a good night's sleep for us lowlanders." He laughs, but it sounds forced.

Despite his words, my father looks well-rested and as handsome as ever in slacks and a dark green quarter-zip sweater, freshly shaven, and his silvering hair neatly combed. But Suzanne looks, well, not great. She has dark slashes under her eyes. The cream turtleneck and black pants she's wearing seem baggy on her. Aren't middle-aged women supposed to gain weight thanks to our friend menopause, not lose it? Avery studies our stepmother closely, too.

Isa stands at the front of the dining room and calls for everyone's attention. She's wearing her uniform of jeans, cowboy boots, and a chambray shirt with the Lazy Dog logo on the chest.

"Hello again, everyone. We hope you had a wonderful morning enjoying some of the ranch's activities. Lunch will be served momentarily. If there are any mix-ups with what you ordered, please let us know right away so we can make it right. I also wanted to let you know that for those who signed up to join us for a sleigh ride this afternoon, please meet at the stables at three o'clock and dress warmly! We'll have blankets and hot beverages, but it gets cold out there. The ride will last about an hour. Thank you and enjoy your meals."

As she's finishing her welcome, Travis slips into the seat next to me, his hair wet and smelling of lavender mint from the fancy shampoo the ranch stocks in the bathrooms. I practically leap into his lap with joy. Like a puppy.

"You're here! Are you okay?" I manage to whisper before grabbing his face and kissing him. He smiles under my lips.

"I'm fine, love. I missed you, though."

"Okay?" Mom says. "Why wouldn't he be okay?"

I open and close my mouth, floundering for something to say.

"Amelia and Travis are never okay unless they're together," Avery says with a subtle wink at us. Jason snorts into his glass of water.

"I'm glad to know that, Amelia," Dad says. "That's exactly what a father wants to hear before his daughter's wedding."

I can see Mom loading her imaginary rifle for an attack, so I start babbling. "Travis and I hate being apart. We work together every day then go home at night, hang out together, and do it all over again the next day. We're great partners, right?"

He puts a hand on my leg to calm me. "Yes, we are. I couldn't imagine living my life without you."

I take a deep breath and relax under his touch.

"That's so sweet," Suzanne says to Travis and me. Her voice is a little weak, but she sounds sincere, so I smile sincerely back.

"It looks like you've picked a good one, Melly," Dad says to me.

"Oh, please, Michael. Don't act like you'd know anything about being a good husband," Mom says. Avery and I freeze, but Dad takes it in stride.

"I wasn't a very good husband to you, Joyce, I'll admit. Or the best father to you girls. But . . . people change." He looks at Suzanne, his expression soft. Her smile falters. And are those tears in her eyes?

Mom looks like she's about to tear into him again, but the waitstaff thankfully swoop by and lay plates in front of us, preventing her from really having a go at him. As they swarm the table, Suzanne, who's seated next to me, leans in.

"Amelia, I'd like to speak to you and your sister in private before the weekend is over. Can we do that? Please?"

I hesitate. The way she'd emphasized the *I* and spoke quietly

enough that my father couldn't hear, made me immediately curious. And wary. But she looks so hopeful, that I say yes.

Still, what could our distant stepmother possibly want to say
to us that our father can't hear?

Chapter Thirteen
SLEIGH RIDE

Travis

I apologize—again—to Amelia as we pull on our winter gear for the afternoon sleigh ride. I feel like all I've done for the past twenty-four hours is thank some people and apologize to others.

"It wasn't your fault. It wasn't anyone's fault," she says. But she seems . . . down. The last thing I want her to feel on our wedding weekend is sad.

I have to admit, as happy as I am to be out of the notorious Laundryland Prison and away from my cellie, Brent, I'm not really in the mood to laugh and talk and drink cider under blankets while being pulled around the ranch by powerful workhorses.

That should sound great, now that I think about it, but I can't muster any enthusiasm for it. I'm tired, and honestly, I'd rather cuddle up with Amelia here in our cabin for a few hours and then go get married. Done.

But instead, we trudge out to the stables looking like colorful snow beasts in all our layers. The temperature has dropped a bit since mid-morning thanks to the cloud cover. Holding hands through our gloves, we join Sarah and Ben on the path heading from the lodge.

"Hey!" Sarah says in greeting. "You guys, this weekend has been *amazing*. I can't wait for this sleigh ride and then the wedding tonight!" Her voice squeaks a bit at the end.

Ben pats her arm. "Me, too, although maybe not quite that excited." He winks at his wife.

"How is Max doing? Having fun so far?" I ask.

"A blast. He went snowshoeing with us this morning." Ben's face grows a little worried over his navy-blue scarf. "Hey, we wanted to ask you—"

Uh oh. Amelia's hand stiffens in mine.

"Is it normal for him to be, well," he glances at Sarah, and then his words rush out. "Mounting everything and everyone he sees? He terrorized a schnauzer yesterday in the lobby, and unless we keep him on a short leash, he's pretty randy with stuff from chair legs to human legs to cats to the toilet seat. It's like he can't tell a girl dog from a stump in the ground."

I laugh, relieved that Ben has a question instead of a request. "We're neutering him next month, right?"

He nods and looks instantly uneasy. Most men do the minute I mention desexing their pets. Sarah, on the other hand, smiles widely. Like most women do.

"Yes. Yes, you are neutering him," she confirms with me. "And not a moment too soon, it seems."

"That should take care of the problem," I say.

Ben rubs his chin. "I hate for him to have to go through it. He's such a stud. I mean, he'd be a great stud. Are male dogs called studs? Or is that horses?"

"Dogs and horses both are called studs," Amelia answers.

I'm proud of how much she's learned since she started her training, first through reading and classwork, then observation and hands-on practice in the Love & Pets mobile.

Sarah shakes her head hard. "We are *not* breeding Max. There are way too many unwanted pets already. Including Labs."

"He'll be fine, Ben, I promise," Amelia says. "Castration," Ben winces as she says the word, "is a really simple surgery, and Travis and I have done lots of the procedures."

"And she does mean a lot," I add. "If you piled up the number of testicles we've removed, it would be a mountain the size of—"

"Okay, okay!" Ben interrupts, his face pained. "I know Max is in good hands with you two. Let's not talk about it anymore."

We all laugh at that, and Sarah louder than anyone.

"Have you seen Brent? Any new signs of Sev Two?" I ask them.

Sarah pulls a face. "No. How a fifty-pound boa constrictor can hide for this long is beyond me. I hope he's not in someone's toilet."

I'm about to tell her that snakes don't tend to seek out toilets when they hide in homes and are more likely to be behind furniture or in warm places like the laundry room, but we've arrived at the stables. And the building happens to be adorned with what else? Balls.

The Christmas variety, that is. The roof that overhangs both the barn and stable doors have the white light strings and round, glittery ornaments hanging from them. Good thing Colorado doesn't get hailstorms in December. Those things would be toast.

In the paddock, five red metal sleighs harnessed to pairs of horses are already assembled with wranglers holding their reins. The Belgian draft horses, from the look of them, stomp the ground with their massive hairy hooves. We grab paper cups of cider and join our friends and family gathered around them, petting the horses' noses while sipping their own hot drinks. I feel my mood lift, especially as I watch Amelia smile and laugh.

After a few minutes, Tobias steps out of the barn looking seriously cowboy cool in his hat, boots, and gray ranch overcoat. His son Tyler is with him, looking every bit the miniature version of his father. It's good to see Ty; we haven't yet this weekend. He seems stronger looking every time we visit, thanks to the cystic fibrosis treatment he's been having in Denver. Isa tells us that although of course it's still a serious disease, he's improving every month.

"Afternoon, everybody. If I haven't already met you, I'm Tobias Coleman, head wrangler and part owner of the Lazy Dog, and this is my boy, Tyler, who's going to help me out today." He smiles down and lays a hand on his son's shoulder. Tyler grins, his blue eyes sparkling. "I hope you're all having a great time so far."

Several people clap and holler, which makes Amelia smile again. Which makes me happy.

"We'll be taking you all out on our sleighs, here, in groups of twelve. Divide yourselves up, and your wranglers will introduce themselves in a minute. But first, a couple of rules about the sleighs and horses."

Tobias lays down the ground rules, which mainly involve staying seated and being careful around the horses' backsides, plus a few others. Amelia and I end up around a sleigh with Avery, Jason, and Joyce, plus Sarah and Ben, and some friends from out of town.

We climb on, sitting along benches that run along the sides of the sleigh, so we face the other half of the group. The wrangler, Jen, a woman in her mid-twenties, passes out blankets to cover our legs. Then she takes the reins again.

"Everyone ready?" When we say we are, she taps the horses lightly on their backs and offers some verbal encouragement, the horses give a massive pull, and we're off.

I'm between Amelia and her mother, who's perched at the end of our row at the back. She wears tight fitting ski pants, a white ski jacket, and way-too-heeled boots, plus a fur hat and huge sunglasses. When the horses pull, she almost falls off with the jolt. I grab her shoulders and right her, and she thanks me with a tight smile.

"I can*not* understand why you two chose a horse ranch of all places for your wedding," she mutters. I pretend not to hear her, instead turning slightly away to listen to Amelia chat animatedly with Sarah and Avery on her other side.

Although I wish Joyce were on a different sleigh, I can't help but enjoy myself. The chill air balances the warmth of the cider plus all of my layers. Red bows and greenery adorn the outsides of the sleighs, and the horses' harnesses are all rigged with jingle bells. Jen provides a nice commentary about the ranch and the surrounding land as we slide smoothly over the snow along well-established tracks.

Seriously, who *wouldn't* choose a dude ranch for their wedding? It's phenomenal out here from the rolling hills covered in snow, to the few peaks we spot through the clouds in the distance, to the cheerful sun peeking out once in a while. Even the changeable weather is part of this place's charm.

"How are you enjoying the weekend, Joyce?" I ask with a smile that's only partially forced. I know full well what I'm going to get—a list of complaints—but maybe then she won't aim them at Amelia later.

Sure enough, she starts with the problems with her room, moves on to the missing snake, the slow service at the bar, the cold, the smelly horses. You name it, and she has a complaint about it. I fix the smile on my face.

"I'm sorry it leaves a little to be desired," I finally say. "Anything you *have* enjoyed?"

"The flower arrangements are gorgeous," she concedes with a grudging note.

I kneel on the bench, probably against the rules, and yell to Ruston and Kenny on the sleigh ahead of us.

Ruston turns. The smaller man is bundled far more than I am; I can barely see his face between his hat and scarf.

"My mother-in-law loves your flowers!" I yell.

"Tell her thank you!" Ruston shouts back. At least, that's what I think he said. His voice is so muffled it's hard to tell.

"She's not your mother-in-law yet, dude," Jason jokes from his spot across from us. "Never know what might happen."

Avery makes an annoyed sound. "Don't jinx them, Jay!"

Joyce ignores the banter, looking away at the view. I study her profile for a moment. It's hard to see how Amelia came from this woman. She's stiff, snobby, negative, and image conscious, all things her daughter is not. But as long as Amelia has her mother in her life, I'll keep trying to be compassionate.

"Did you hear what happened with James and Mika after the barbecue last night?" Jason says, asking about shared friends of ours who are dating. I shake my head. Amelia and I spent so long talking with people after lunch, we barely had time to change and get here. He makes an explosion sound and spreads his hands apart.

As he tells me about their dust up, and the epic makeup this morning at breakfast, I'm also half listening to Amelia tell Sarah and Ben all about my ordeal in the laundry room. To hear her version, it was kind of funny. No, okay. It really had been funny, but I wish it had been a funny story about someone else.

"Hang on, folks," Jen says. She pulls the horses to a slow halt and Joyce rocks unsteadily again. If she'd sit further back and put both feet on the ground instead of crossing her legs, she wouldn't be so off balance. Appropriate footwear might have helped, too.

We're stopped in a wide, snow-covered field where we're given the chance to handfeed some of the ranch's off-duty horses from the hay bales piled on the ground. With their powerful bodies and shiny coats, their thick manes and swishing tails, they're magnificent. I feed a few, then sit back to enjoy watching Amelia interact confidently with them. We mostly treat small pets in our practice, but we keep my buffalo, Chuck, and the occasional foster horse at our home stables, and she's learned to care for them like a veteran ranch hand.

Along with Chuck, Doug, Daisy, and the doggy band, the Four Horsemen, we also have my pre-Amelia menagerie of one cat (our other died last year), a dwindling group of leopard frogs, a whiptail lizard, and an aging sunbeam snake. We'd probably take on more rescues, but we work so much, it wouldn't be fair. We have a pet sitter stop by every day as it is, and that gets expensive.

Avery cajoles her mother into holding out a handful of hay for a particularly majestic paint horse who approaches the sleigh, but Joyce gets the jitters and drops it before the horse can take it. Ranch life, even for a weekend, really doesn't seem to suit her.

After fifteen minutes, the wrangler asks us to sit again, and with another strong pull, the sleigh lurches forward.

Joyce screams, and as I turn her way, I realize she wasn't quite seated yet. I reach out, ready to grab her, but it's too late. She tumbles right off the bench, through the open back of the moving sleigh, and into the snow.

Chapter Fourteen

GRANDMA GOT RUN OVER BY A REINDEER

Amelia

"Stop the sleigh!" Travis yells to Jen as he vaults off the back of the sleigh . . . where Mom no longer sits. Jason joins him, and as the sleigh slides to a stop, I scuttle off the back too, afraid of what I'll see behind us.

Mom is sprawled in the snow, and Travis and Jason squat on either side of her. After a moment, they help her to sit. She cradles her left wrist in her right hand.

"Oh no," I whisper to Avery, who jumped off beside me. "Is she hurt?"

"I'm not sure, but . . . look at her coat."

Avery groans. Mom's beautiful and expensive-looking white coat, which she told me she'd bought especially for the weekend, is covered in horse manure. It flakes off her like scabs, leaving poopy stains behind.

We hurry to her side.

"Mom? Are you okay?" I kneel in front of her, careful not to put my knee in anything but snow.

"No! Of course, I'm not okay. Look at my wrist!" Mom wails. She holds out her gloved left hand. Her wrist looks normal at first glance. Her sunglasses, on the other hand, are askew on her face, and her hat fell off. Onto a pile of manure, of course. Jason scoops it up and shakes it out but has the good sense not to try to put it back on Mom's head.

"May I look at your wrist?" Travis asks .

Mom nods, so he gently slips her glove off. The skin of her hand and wrist are pale. Mom's always been fair skinned. Nothing abnormal there. As he pushes the sleeve of her coat and sweater up, she moans a little, but there's no bruising or obvious swelling. He turns it over to look at the underside and probes softly with his fingers, watching her face. She winces.

"Looks okay so far," he says. "It might be a sprain rather than a break."

"Well, what do you know? You're an animal doctor, not a people doctor," Mom says through gritted teeth.

Avery makes an angry sound from beside Jason. "That's gratitude for you."

"Oh, hush up, Avery, I'm in pain," Mom says.

Travis doesn't respond, but his jaw clenches slightly.

"I can call up a Jeep from the ranch," Jen says, pulling out a walkie talkie from the front pocket of her heavy-duty coat, "if you think we need it."

I look to Travis, pointedly ignoring my mother's whimpers. My body alternately boils and freezes with fury over my mother's rudeness to him. And to me, too, if you include the whole weekend.

He's studying her wrist. "I think it should be x-rayed to be on the safe side. Would you call that Jeep please?" he asks the wrangler. She steps away to make the call. "I can take her."

"No." Avery's voice is as firm as hard-packed earth. "I'll take her."

"I'll do it, babe," Jason says. "You're the maid of honor."

"But you're the best man," she says back to him.

"We'll take her," a male voice says from beside us. It's Kenny. A small crowd has grown from the other sleighs, which stopped when they heard and saw the commotion. I throw my old work colleague and friend a grateful but warning look. If my mother is mean to Kenny and Ruston too, that's it.

Mom's expression is unhappy. "But my daughters—"

"Need to get ready for the main event tonight, Joyce," Ruston says breezily, like he already has everything figured out. "And we need to get you x-rayed and treated at urgent care and then back and looking fabulous for your role as mother of the bride tonight, right? C'mon, we'll make sure you're very well taken care of."

While Ruston chats at, more than with, Mom, about how they'll handle everything and that it all will be okay, I hug Kenny. "Thank you so, so much."

"You're welcome, Princess." Then he lowers his voice and leans near my ear. "Don't worry, we'll deliver the Wicked Witch of the West to the wedding on time." He winks solemnly.

The sound of an engine grows from the direction of the ranch. Within a minute, a Jeep pulls up beside us, Addie at the wheel. This is all she needs, I think. Another problem with our weekend. It's all *we* need.

I turn to my mother, but I don't know what to say. My natural instinct is to worry and show concern when someone's injured, but honestly? She doesn't deserve it.

"I hope it's not broken, Mom." My voice is stiff; I'm having a hard time putting any real concern behind my words.

Addie and Travis help my suddenly frail-looking mother into the passenger seat of the Jeep, while Ruston and Kenny climb into the backseat. I blow them a kiss. If my mother sees me and thinks it's for her, fine. But it isn't. I'm sorry she was hurt, but she's officially hit my limit of patience and under-standing.

"Keep your wrist above your heart as much as you can to help with swelling," Travis advises, and Mom nods. Then Addie pulls away, and the Jeep moves slowly along the trail back toward the ranch.

"Let's load up again, folks," Jen says. "And please, stay seated and keep a hand on the handrails for me, okay?"

Travis helps me up onto the sleigh again and we take our seats. The day is as beautiful as before, but the mood is more somber now. Of course, Mom ruined it. Not due to the accident but because of her consistently negative attitude.

Avery nudges me. "Hey, don't let this get to you. She'll be fine and probably back and complaining about the ceremony before we know it."

I nod, but I can't find the humor in her words. I lean against Travis' shoulder. "You didn't deserve that."

"It's okay, she's right. I'm not a doctor."

"But you were trying to help. It infuriates me that she never sees that in other people. No matter what, everything is always about *her*." I keep my voice low, but it's shaking, and my body feels as tense as a rubber band pulled as far as it can go. "No wonder Dad left her."

Travis takes my gloved hand and kisses it, and then he puts an arm around me and holds me close. "Try to let it go, love. Life is short, and she's your—"

"I don't *care* if she's my mother anymore," I whisper furiously, close to tears. "I'm sick of being respectful because she's my mother. I'm going to tell her I don't want to see her anymore after this weekend. Because that's how I feel."

He squeezes my shoulder. "I understand, and of course, I'll support whatever you decide. But give yourself the rest of the weekend to think about it, okay?"

I swallow and take a long, cleansing breath. "Hey, Jason, do you still have that flask on you?"

He grins and tugs the small silver container out of his jacket's chest pocket. I pour a bit into my ice-cold cider and take a sip. I don't dare drink more than a shot before the wedding, but the bourbon goes down smoothly. Avery takes a swig out of the flask, too, and hands it back to Jason.

My eyes lock with my older sister's. She has a different relationship with our mother—always has. It's been, basically, on Avery's terms. Which meant I often had to pick up the slack when our mother needed things. But maybe it's time for both Avery and me to insist on our own terms, and Mom will have to deal with it.

Starting with the decision I need to make now. Kenny will completely understand my choice, I know, because he's a true friend.

I take out my phone and pull up the messaging app. *Hey Dad, will you walk me down the aisle this evening?*

The reply comes back in less than a minute.

Of course, Amelia. I would love to.

Chapter Fifteen

WINTER SONG

Travis

"Are you sure you're all right?" I ask Amelia as we stand on the path beside the Kissing Bridge. She'd been very quiet for the remainder of the sleigh ride after Joyce was driven away. She wasn't smiling again either.

"I'm fine. In fact, I feel really good for the first time this weekend."

"Because you won't have to see me for the next few hours?" I tease. I'm getting a drink with Jason and a few of our guy friends at the bar before going to Jason and Avery's room to get ready for the ceremony. I'd hung my suit and put my shoes in their closet yesterday and gave Jason the rings for safekeeping. Hopefully—please, Lord—he still has them.

Amelia and I won't see each other again until she walks down the aisle and stands beside me to say the words that will make me the happiest guy on earth.

She scoffs. "Of course not. I just feel, I don't know, ready. Ready to start my life with you. Ready to become Amelia

Brewer. Ready to be your wife instead of only someone's daughter or sister or girlfriend. Ready to build something fresh and exciting and exclusively ours."

She pulls me close and kisses me deeply. Her lips, usually soft, even hesitant at times, are insistent.

I grab a breath, my heart pounding, and smooth her hair down her back. "That sounded like it could be your vow. Want to hear mine?"

"No. Not yet. Save it for later."

"You sure? It's a good one. I think you'll like it." I touch my mouth to hers again.

"I'll love it. That's not the problem. But I want to be as awed and surprised and stirred as everyone else when they hear it."

"Stirred?" I pull her close into my body. "How stirred do you think you might be?"

She smiles seductively, sending my blood speeding faster through my veins. "That depends on how convincing you are. But I'll be sure to let you know later . . . after the ceremony . . . when we're back in our cabin with the fire lit and Doug and Daisy snoozing in their crate."

"I wish we were there now." And I really mean it. "Hey, speaking of the pugs, do you want me to check on Doug before I head to Jason's room?" She'd told me about his bout of nausea.

"I'll call you if he's any worse. He seemed fine before we went out for the sleigh ride. I'll walk them and play with them while Avery and I are hanging out."

Amelia and her sister are having a glass of champagne in our cabin before getting ready.

"All right, well, I love you, I can't wait to see you in your dress, and . . . I can't wait to put that ring on your finger and make you mine."

"Back at you, Doctor Travis." She winks and turns to head up the hill.

Damn, I love this woman.

After making sure she gets inside okay, I walk to the lodge. I need to use the restroom before meeting the boys in the bar. But as I admire the sunlight glittering against the peaks to the south, beyond the lodge and activity center, I hear shouting voices and a dog's frantic barking.

Don't get involved, Travis. There are obviously people with the dog, and they can handle it. Don't. Get. Involved.

I don't listen to myself, of course.

Instead, I take the cleared walkway between the lodge and activity center and pass the sprawling patio and fire pit on one side and the drained and covered outdoor pool on the other. A couple of people are in the distance, but I don't see the barking dog.

Grateful for my heavy-duty snow boots, I trek across a snow-field that they must have crossed to get to where they are. When I get close enough, I shout to let them know I'm coming. The guy turns and waves.

"Doc!" It's Logan, one of our clients, which means the woman must be Stevie. Which means the dog barking, who I still can't see, must be Bean, their spirited border collie.

"Everything okay?" I yell as I get closer.

"It's Bean," he says. "We came out here to throw the frisbee for her, but, well, look."

He points, but I can't quite see what's he gesturing to yet. As I pass Stevie, I realize she's crying. Then, I finally see Bean.

Wet and shaking, a frisbee by her feet, she stands in the middle of what looks like a frozen pond wearing a green and blue plaid sweater and dog boots made for playing in the snow. It's difficult to tell there's a body of water here, because it's covered in a layer of snow, but there's a watery hole in the ice right in front of Bean that she must have recently fallen into.

Stevie's eyes are bloodshot, and her face is drained of color. She digs in her pocket to pull out a tissue.

"We . . . we were trying to help her burn some energy before the wedding tonight, but we didn't realize there was a pond or lake or whatever here, and I threw the disc really far, and Bean jumped onto the ice and it cracked and she went through. She pulled herself out, but we can't get to her because we don't want to fall in ourselves or cause the ice to break up, and she's afraid to move."

Stevie and Bean had joined a disc dog club this past summer, and the border collie is obsessed, I'd heard.

"Okay. Let me think about this." I walk cautiously to what I think is the edge of the pond and brush away a layer of snow on top of a lump poking up above the rest of the ground. "Well, here you go."

It's a sign that warns that the water freezes in winter and isn't safe.

"Not much help now," Logan says. He has his arm around Stevie, attempting to comfort her, but her eyes are glued to Bean, who whimpers forlornly.

"Try not to worry," I say. "She has a good, thick coat and it's not quite freezing."

"But how do we . . . get to her?" Stevie asks through tears.

That is the question. "Have you tested the ice?"

"It wouldn't hold my weight." Logan nods and points to an area where a set of footsteps goes down to the pond and then back up.

"We tried calling to her, but she's terrified," Stevie says. "She won't budge."

I notice she's wearing a backpack. "What do you have in there? Anything edible for a dog?"

She shakes her head. "A water bottle, a protein shake, my wallet, and another disc. We always carry a couple in case one cracks."

"Let's get it out," I say. She scrambles in her backpack and tugs it free. The yellow disc is bright against the white snow. Bean's eyes follow the disc, but she doesn't move. "Okay, now try throwing it."

Stevie pulls her arm back as if to throw to Bean, but I yelp. "Not to her! That way," I point to the field behind us, "so she'll hopefully follow it, avoid the hole in the ice, and get back to dry land on her own."

"Oh, right!" Stevie says. "Beanie weenie, look! See the disc?" She waves it around to catch the border collie's attention. Bean tilts her head and picks one foot up, and then the other. "Come get it, girl!" Stevie slings the disc into the field. It flies, falls, and disappears into the top layer of snow.

Bean stays put.

"Right." What to try next? I inch back to the edge of the pond. "I'll try to get across and get her."

"No, Travis, it's too dangerous. And you have to get married in like . . . an hour and forty-five minutes." Logan's an accountant, so he's very . . . precise. "I'll try."

"No!" Stevie says. "I'm not letting either of you do it. I weigh the least, so I'll try."

"Stevie—" Logan says.

"We don't have time to argue about this," she says. "I'm getting Bean back." Shoulders set, she walks to the edge of the pond.

"Maybe try easing out on your belly." I saw something about that on a nature survival show once. By distributing your weight, you're less likely to break the ice.

"Keep your backpack on so we can grab it and haul you out if we have to. And please be careful." Logan looks tense as we follow and hover behind her.

Stevie gets on her knees, and then puts her hands out and wriggles a little at a time onto the ice. Her body pushes the snow away, revealing the thin ice below. The surface makes a creaking, cracking sound, but it doesn't collapse. Bean whines, her eyes on her mistress.

Logan leans in, ready to grab Stevie's pack if the ice cracks, but so far, so good. She uses her gloved hands to pull herself bit by bit toward her dog. Her upper body is on the ice. Now her thighs, her knees, and her feet.

As she nears the hole Bean created when she leapt to catch the disc, she hesitates and peers back at us. "I'm scared."

"You can do it," Logan says, his voice calm and expression tender. These two have been friends since childhood and finally got together a few months ago. But they'd loved each other for years as far as Amelia and I could tell.

Stevie focuses on Bean and slides farther. The ice crackles again, Bean barks, and Logan and I freeze.

Stevie reaches out her hand and calls to Bean. "C'mon, Beanie. Come, sweet girl."

Bean takes a cautious step, eyeing the hole in the ice, then another step. Her thin, soggy tail wags hesitantly. Stevie encourages her, and as Bean reaches her the ice gives a loud crack.

"Hold still!" I yell. "Don't move."

But it's too late. The ice gives, and Stevie and Bean both go in with a splash.

"Stevie!" Logan almost falls in trying to reach her, so I yank him back by his coat, and we land in the snow on our butts. In a flash, we're on our feet again. And . . .

So is Stevie.

Because the pond is only knee deep.

Here by the edge, at least. Logan and I look at each other and laugh with relief combined with disbelief. Stevie, now soaked, lifts Bean out of the water and wades to the edge.

Logan helps them out of the pond, and Bean jumps down to shake her whole body vigorously, sending water droplets flying.

At least now I can help. "I'll run with Bean to the lodge, get her toweled off and warm by the fire, and check her paws. Logan, you help Stevie back. Sound good?"

"Thank . . . you!!" Stevie says through clattering teeth.

I consider carrying Bean, but we can get there faster separately, and the exertion will help warm her. "Let's go, Bean!"

Awkwardly, thanks to my snow boots, I lope toward the main building, calling to the dog as I go. When Stevie encourages her, she follows, bursting through the snow behind me like a black and white plow.

A few seconds later, she stops and digs her head into the snow. I slow.

"Bean?"

When she pulls her head out, the yellow disc in her teeth, I have to laugh again. I've probably missed Jason and the others at the bar given the number of times I heard my cell phone ring, but honestly, I'd rather have been here, helping my clients and patient, than anywhere else.

Promise or no promise.

Wedding day or no wedding day.

Chapter Sixteen
MY CHRISTMAS TREE IS HUNG WITH TEARS

Amelia

Avery takes a long sip of her champagne and puts her slippered feet up on the middle of the couch next to my slippered feet. We've showered, we're in robes, and our hair is air-drying. We have about forty-five minutes to relax, and then we'll need to get ourselves ready for the ceremony.

My nerves need this drink like a dying houseplant needs water. Unless the houseplant has been overwatered and that's why it's dying. Then it probably doesn't need it. Anyway—I need this drink.

I pet Doug and Daisy, who are curled up between us on the couch, while trying to focus on and enjoy the warmth of the fire burning in the gas fireplace, the dryness of the wine, and the bubbles as they fizz down my throat. I'll only have one glass, I promise myself. Along with several of these chocolate-covered strawberries that Travis and I were never in the same place long enough to eat. I reach for one now.

Avery lifts her phone imperiously. "Okay, we'll read Mom's

text once, and then we aren't going to worry about it, got it?" She clears her throat and reads it silently. She raises an eyebrow at me. "They did an x-ray and it's not broken. Probably sprained. But she'll need to wear a wrist brace. And she's in pain. A lot of it. That's not a surprise."

Mom's never been tough when it comes to injuries. "What else did she say?"

Avery scans the text again. "Nothing you need to hear. This isn't our fault. We didn't *push* her off the sleigh, after all."

I nod again, but guilt rises along with a few stray champagne bubbles. "I feel bad that we didn't take her." My voice comes out very small and weak and timid, like a mouse.

"Amelia, no. Mom has been a . . . I won't say it, you know what she's been . . . this whole weekend. She's demanding, complaining, rude to Travis, doesn't appreciate anything we do, and yet expects us, you especially, to cater to her twenty-four seven. You shouldn't feel bad. She's lucky she was invited."

I nod, but the self-reproach stays with me. She's our mother, and she's been there for us in her own way, even if her own way isn't the loving, kind way we expect from mothers.

"It's too late now anyway, I guess," I say.

"Damn right it is. We're a glass of champagne into the calm before the wedding storm, and we're going to enjoy it." With a defiant toss of her damp hair, Avery fills our glasses up. I sip mine pensively.

"Seriously, forget Mom. She'll be fine. Let's talk about your makeup. Do you want a bolder eye or a bolder lip? Or both? No, that'll be too much. I vote bold eye, and a soft pink lipstick. Or I can—"

A knock on the door interrupts her musing. The pugs leap off the couch and attack the door, barking. Avery hops up, puts her drink down, and tightens her robe around her waist.

"I've got it. Whoever this is, they can't come in. They can see you at the wedding. Including your groom, if it's him. Especially if it's . . ." She opens the door, keeping Doug and Daisy back with a strategically placed foot, but her voice falters. ". . . him. Suzanne. Hi. Is everything okay?"

"Yes . . . well . . . for now. May I come in? There's something I'd really like to speak with you and your sister about." Suzanne's voice is soft, and she sounds frail again.

Avery glances back at me questioningly. I nod and sit up, putting my feet back on the ground. I have no idea what she wants to tell us. Honestly, with all the, er, excitement of Mom's injury, I'd forgotten Suzanne asked to talk to us. I hadn't even told my sister about it.

I call the dogs back to sit by my feet, and after Avery takes Suzanne's coat and offers her a drink, which she refuses, I invite our stepmother to take the comfy leather chair nearest to the fireplace. She settles herself, her hands in her lap. They're so white and thin, I can see every vein running across like thin blue rivulets. Avery and I retake our seats on the couch and wait.

Suzanne swallows nervously. "Avery, Amelia . . . I want to start by apologizing that I didn't make more of an effort with you since I married your father. You were almost adults when we met, but that's no excuse. I could have done a better job getting to know you."

Avery sort of shrugs and nods. She's not one to pretend she doesn't understand what someone means or that everything's okay when it isn't. But I am.

"We understand, Suzanne. Our parents' divorce was . . . rough, as you probably know. Dad met you pretty soon after, and Avery and I had our hands full with Mom." And . . . she would've been hurt if we'd started a relationship with Suzanne back then. Hurt means furious when it comes to our mother. We'd left it alone.

She nods. "Still, I wish I'd gotten to know you two better. Really. More than you know."

Avery glances at me, and I see the same confusion on her face that I feel inside.

"It's not too late. Is it?" I ask.

"Yeah, Mom's doing better with everything now—I mean, for our mom," Avery rolls her eyes, "and Dad seems really happy. So . . . why are you telling us this—"

"Now?" Suzanne finishes for her. She rubs her palms lightly on her slacks as if they're sweaty. "Because . . . I have stage four breast cancer. And the treatment is not going very well."

I gasp and shrink into my robe, while Avery sits ramrod straight. Neither of us speak for a moment.

My sister shakes herself loose from the shock first. "I'm really sorry, Suzanne. How long have you been in treatment? And why didn't Dad tell us?"

"This is my second bout with it. The first was before I met your father. But it came back about nine months ago, more aggressively than before. As for Michael, I asked him not to tell you. I knew how busy you two were with planning the wedding. And I wouldn't have told you now, but we're catching an earlier plane home in the morning."

"Are you okay?" I grimace as the words come out. "I mean, I know you're not, but is anything wrong right now?"

"I'm struggling with the altitude and my medications. But listen, I didn't come here to talk about my illness. Honestly, I didn't. I came because of your father." She licks her lips. "When I'm . . . gone . . . he'll need you girls."

Avery stiffens again, and I know how she's feeling. He needs us? *We* needed *him* after the divorce, but he was too busy with work and his new relationship with Suzanne. I put a hand on my sister's, trying to make it subtle. Suzanne notices both the stiffening and the hand.

"I know it's a lot to ask given . . . everything. But he loves you both so much, and he's very proud of all you've accomplished. He talks about you all the time, stories about when you were young, and he has pictures of you all around the house. He has some friends that he can lean on, of course, but I know he'd rather spend time with you. If you'll allow him to." She sighs.

"Maybe I'm not the one who should be asking you this. But I hope you'll consider it."

I glance at Avery. "We will. I mean we'll think about it. And I'm so sorry again, Suzanne."

"I am, too. I wish things were different—" She looks out the window, swallowing back tears, but a moment later she smiles and stands. "And now I'll leave you two to get ready for the ceremony. Thank you for hearing me out." She stands and pulls on her coat and gloves to leave.

"Suzanne," I say as she moves to the door. When she pauses, I hug her.

Avery and I have had our problems with our father, but I'd always suspected I might like our stepmom if I'd had the chance to get to know her. And Dad . . . he will be crushed. Suzanne seems to be the love of his life. I wish our mom had been, but sometimes that's not how life works.

"Thank you, Amelia," she whispers, her eyes glassy again. She smiles at Avery, who smiles cautiously back, and she's gone.

Chapter Seventeen
ROCKING AROUND THE CHRISTMAS TREE

Amelia

Avery and I don't talk much about what Suzanne told us. We don't have the time, or frankly, emotional energy for it. Instead, as soon our stepmother leaves, I'm sucked into a wedding blender of dress, hair, makeup, and snow boots. We'll carry our heels over to the lodge with us.

But Avery had said this much: "He doesn't deserve us." And after a moment, she'd added, "He might not deserve her, either."

I don't know about that. All I know is that my brain is completely fogged by Suzanne's news, my nerves, fear, and the champagne.

When I'd pictured our wedding day up to now, it had always been like a beautiful dream. Our friends, family, clients, pets, and gorgeous holiday decorations, all set amidst the stunning back-drop of a dude ranch in the Colorado mountains on a sunny, wintry day.

Instead, it's kind of gray. Two people have needed emergency care—including Mom. Travis got stuck overnight in the laundry room. Severus the Second is still missing, and Suzanne is terminally ill. No, seriously, what else can go wrong?

I try not to dwell on these negative thoughts as Avery and I take Doug and Daisy out for a last wring out before we head down to the lodge. Addie said she would text when everyone was gathered and ready, so that we're not milling around with guests before the ceremony starts.

But my low mood is hard to wish away as Avery and I wait side by side on the couch in front of the fire, dresses on, the dogs in the sweet holiday sweaters I'd bought them for today. I scratch them, concentrating on their firm bodies and sweet faces.

"Are you ready for this?" Avery asks.

I blink. "I think so. I mean, I know I'm ready to marry Travis. I've been ready for years. At this point, I just want it to go smoothly." I pause. "Aves?"

She raises an eyebrow.

"Thank you for being here for me. From the Tim days—"

"Ugh, don't mention that man."

"To helping Doug, to meeting Travis, to supporting me while I went back to school, to pet sitting for us over the years when I know you aren't a huge dog lover, to trying to manage Mom. I'm grateful for all of it."

She slings an arm around me, and I rest my head carefully on her shoulder. I don't want to smear makeup or mess up my hair. "You're my sister and my best friend, Amelia. I love you more than ice cream and wine."

"Wow. Ice cream *and* wine?"

She thinks about it. "Definitely ice cream. Wine might be an even match up."

I snort and she laughs.

"No snorting allowed in that wedding dress. Not when you look so amazing. You're a winter wedding goddess."

Affectionately, I smooth the soft duchess satin of my dress, admiring the simplicity of the design all over again. It has capped sleeves, a V neckline, and very little embellishment. Avery had styled my hair in a loose, low bun. I love how it all came together. Simple. Like I'd hoped this weekend would be.

I snort again, making my sister scowl.

"What did I say about snorting?" she asks.

I snort a third time, and she must figure if you can't beat 'em, join 'em, because she snorts a few times, too. The dogs even get in on the action, sensing our silliness, but it's not all that hard for pugs to snort and look silly. Avery and I are laughing within seconds.

In the midst of the snort-fest, the text comes in. She holds up her phone. "It's go time."

The anxiety crashes back over me as we yank on our coats, scoop up the dogs, ruck up our skirts, and hustle down to the lodge. As we slip inside the main doors, everything looks perfect. Our guests are seated in rows of white folding chairs facing the windows at the far end and listening to our friend Raoul play his guitar to one side of the lobby. The fireplace is lit with a warm, crackling log fire. Travis, Jason, and the minister stand in front of the stunning Christmas tree, the phenomenal mountain views on full display behind them . . . minus a few mountains thanks to the clouds.

Isa, Addie, Dad, and Ruston wait for us inside the doors. We step to the side into an alcove where the guests can't see. Doug and Daisy shake themselves noisily, and Avery hushes them.

Isa and Addie quietly squeal as they collect our coats and boots. "You look gorgeous, Amelia!" Isa whispers. "So beautiful."

"Travis will pee his pants when he sees you!" Addie says. "Everything should be ready. We're going to go sit with Tobias and Tyler. Good luck!"

I hug them, and they tiptoe off. Ruston hands me my bouquet—a traditional bunch of red roses, my favorite. He kisses my cheek and whispers, "You look fantastic, Amelia. Like a princess."

He winks at me. Kenny's old nickname for me, from our days

at the l-awful offices of Hand, Hart, and Butz, had stuck a little too well. I bring my nose close to the bouquet. The scent is so delicate and sweet I can almost taste it. It would be weird for the bride to nibble on her wedding flowers, right?

"I'm so glad you all made it back in time. Is Mom here?" I ask.

"In the flesh." Ruston peeks around at the backs of the guests and points her out in the front row. "My word, that woman is a handful."

I hug him. "You and Kenny were this princess's knights in shining armor today."

Ruston smiles broadly before strolling out to join Kenny, wherever he's sitting.

"Girls, you look beautiful. Absolutely beautiful." Dad steps forward and hugs Avery, and then me. Now's not the time to talk to him about Suzanne, of course, but my heart hurts for him. Avery's eyes roam his face, looking for signs of the sorrow that must be there.

When I look closely, I see them. The lines on his forehead are deeper, his hair is thinner than the last time I saw him. Even his eyes seem set deeper in his face, as if they've sunk.

I kiss his cheek. "Thank you for being here, Dad."

He looks surprised, but he covers it quickly. "Thank you for asking me. I'm honored to take this walk with you. Travis is a good man. You've chosen well."

My heart swells. Even though I quit relying on Dad years ago, and I don't need anyone's approval to marry Travis, I realize I desperately wanted at least one of my parents' validation now. I blink back tears. No crying later, I hear Avery say as she applied my makeup, you'll smear your mascara.

As if on cue, Raoul starts playing the wedding march, a stripped-down version that's perfect for the elegant but rustic setting. As he does, the doors open and Bea and Seb slip in with Fluff in her carrier. They look flushed and wind swept, as if they'd rushed to get here. Now that I think about it, I haven't seen them since last night.

They wave and go to find seats, and I lean down to scratch Doug and Daisy. "Ready, you two?"

The pugs dance on their paws and lick their snouts. Ready. Avery takes both leashes, and I take Dad's arm.

"Are *you* ready, Amelia?" he asks me as we walk to the back of the aisle through the chairs.

My eyes find Travis. In his charcoal suit, his shiny hair hanging free to brush his shoulders, and with a soft smile growing on his lips as he takes me in, I know. I am ready. Ready to be his wife and to love and cherish him for all of our days. I nod to my father, and we take the first step.

But that's as far as we get.

A few feet ahead with Avery, Doug lunges to their left, yanking her into the guest at the end of the last aisle, which turns out to be our clients, Stevie and Logan, and their dog, Bean, who looks freshly bathed and brushed. Doug and Bean sniff each other's butts and whine, wagging their tails furiously. Avery tugs Doug back into the aisle.

"I'm so sorry!" Stevie whispers to us.

We all move again, but not three seconds later Avery makes a horrified sound. Max is on top of Daisy in the aisle, doing what intact males do best. Everyone watches with open mouths and wide eyes—and a few giggles. Sarah and Ben look mortified as they get Max back under control and we all start out again.

My eyes find Mom. She shakes her head, her mouth a thin line. She doesn't need to say a word; I can hear her thoughts perfectly well.

Why did we allow guests to bring pets? It's the stupidest idea she's ever heard.

But as I look around, and listen to the quiet whines, mews, and even a squawk, I know why. This wedding is a reflection of Travis and me. Pets are what brought us together. They're our livelihood. They're our family, and their humans are our friends.

Sure, they're trouble, and maybe they don't mix very well with a formal event. But our wedding was never meant to be formal. It's . . . us. Travis and me.

I relax, laugh, and meet my fiancé's eyes. He looks as amused as I suddenly feel. And then I'm beside him, and my dad's kissing my cheek, and Travis and I face the minister.

Honestly, I can't really recall much of the ceremony. It's a happy blur punctuated by a few barks, whines, and hisses. What I do remember is Travis' beautiful face and shining eyes. I hear the melody of his voice as we exchange vows, smell the soap on his skin, feel the roughness of his hard-working hands in mine, and finally taste his lips as they press against mine—as man and wife.

One other thing: I can barely fit the ring on his finger thanks to a chunky Band-Aid on his knuckle that I hadn't noticed before. I narrow my eyes in question, but he gives me a *tell you later* look.

People cheer and clap after we kiss, which turns out to be the exact wrong thing to do. The three Z's, their leashes previously in young Tyler's hands, tear away from him and launch playful attacks on Doug and Daisy. Avery and Jason drop the pugs' leashes and the five dogs roll around, growling and barking. Black and white Persian cats—Romeo and Juliet—dash across the lobby with the schnauzer, Skye, on their tails. Kathleen and Joe chase them, calling to them futilely.

As Travis, Tobias, Tyler, and Jason struggle to separate the skirmishing dogs, Max the Lab streaks up the aisle past us, the minister, and the tangle of dogs at our feet, and with a toothy smile of relief, lifts his leg on the Christmas tree, including spraying down some of our wedding gifts arranged below the branches.

My mother screams, and I whirl in her direction. She points at the tree with her splinted hand. "The . . . the . . . the . . . snake!"

Sure enough, something long, smooth, and definitely

reptilian is wrapped around the tree's trunk like a huge strand of brownish-green tinsel. The minister hops away, robes flapping. I scoop Doug up, crushing my bouquet, and step back, right onto Travis' foot with my heel. He yelps in pain.

Brent trots forward.

"Sev! There are you are! Have you been here the whole time, buddy?" He grins at Travis and me. "Found him! Oh, and hey, congrats you two. *Great* wedding."

Chapter Eighteen
IT'S THE MOST WONDERFUL TIME OF THE YEAR

Amelia

"Everybody! Calm down!" Isa stands beside us, shouting and waving her arms. "Please! Cool it!"

After a moment, people quit screaming, catch their escaped pets, get them on leashes or in carriers, or in Brent's case, wrapped around his neck, and we all go relatively quiet. The humans, anyway.

One manicured hand on her chest, Isa takes a deep breath. "Well, *that* was exciting." Everyone laughs, some a little shakily. "And with that, er, wild ending, congratulations to Mr. and Mrs. Travis and Amelia Brewer!"

Doug and Daisy whine as our guests clap. The round of applause ends quickly when the pets start howling, mewling, and screeching again. Isa waits before speaking again.

"Travis and Amelia were kind enough to welcome your pets to the ceremony, but in the interest of having a safe and, er, hygienic reception, let's take a short break to return all pets to their crates in your rooms and cabins."

As a healthy chunk of our guests head off in different directions, Tobias and Tyler approach us wearing identical bashful expressions.

"I'm sorry the Z's got away from me," Tyler says. "They do that sometimes."

"That's okay, Ty. They just wanted to say hello to Doug and Daisy." Travis—my husband! —lets go of my hand and squats down so he's at eye level with the boy. "Seen any good vintage Broncos games with your grandpa lately?"

While Travis and Tyler catch up, I thank Tobias. "It's been an amazing weekend despite the . . . mishaps."

The wrangler shakes his head and smiles ruefully. "Mishaps is a kind way to put it. But I can't count how many folks have asked if we allow pets the rest of the year, too. When I tell them we do, within reason, they've all said they want to visit again soon. Maybe we should pay you two instead." He winks at me.

When Tobias leads Tyler and the Z's away, Travis takes my hands again and faces me. "Hey, Mrs. Brewer. I think I'll take the pugs back to the room, Mrs. Brewer. If that's okay with you . . . Mrs. Brewer. Can you tell I like the sound of that?"

I kiss him, my lips lingering on his. "I'm getting that idea."

His gaze intensifies for a moment, as if he'd like to call me by my new name in private, but then he whistles to the dogs who follow him toward the coat racks Addie and Isa set up by the doors.

Avery hugs me then. "That wedding was so . . . you and Travis."

I bite my lip. "Is that a good thing?"

She grins. "It's a beautiful thing. Really, Mel."

Dad hugs me next, congratulating me. Are those tears in his eyes? Suzanne stands a little way away, talking to Sarah, who must have sent bad boy Max back to their room with Ben.

"Dad?" I take his hand and Avery's. "Suzanne told us her . . . news."

He looks shocked. And instantly sad. "She did?"

"You should have told us sooner," Avery says.

"But we want you to know," I hurry along before she scolds him, "that we'll be here for you. When you need us." My sister nods.

Dad bows his head for a moment. "I'm a lucky man to have such wonderful daughters. Know this: I wish I could go back in time and be a different kind of father." He pauses, his jaw clenching. "But since I can't, I want to be a different father now, if you'll let me. I've learned a lot the last few years. Mainly, that I should keep close the people I value, and work hard to earn their love. Please let me try to earn yours."

I wipe a leaking tear as he kisses each of our cheeks tenderly.

When Travis returns, we're swept along to our table to eat the delicious meal Wanda, Myra, and their staff prepared, to talk, to drink, to talk, to cut and eat the wedding cake, and to talk. And all along, I hear hilarious stories about which pet did what during the ceremony.

One thing is clear: ours is a wedding that won't be easily forgotten.

"Amelia?" Mom leans over my chair and drapes her arm around me. From her demeanor, she's had a few glasses of wine. "I'm sorry."

Having that word issue from her mouth is a shock. I stand so I can hear her better, and she fingers her wine glass nervously.

"I . . . haven't been on my best behavior this weekend." She lowers her voice. "I was upset that you were getting married. You know how I feel about the institution in general, and . . . I don't want your heart to be broken." Like hers had been, she doesn't say. But I know that's what she means. "And then I was annoyed that you chose to get married here instead of at home, that you'd selected such a rural venue, that you'd invited your father, and that you and your sister didn't take me to the hospital yourselves earlier, among other things." She counts her complaints out on the fingers of her good hand. As if I need to hear them again. "But I want you to know that Travis has been very kind to me this afternoon, checking on me and making sure my wine glass is full. And I know you love him, and he loves you." Her lips thin. "For now, anyway. And that makes me . . . happy." She tosses her hair back and takes a drink, as if that admission made her as uncomfortable as it had astonished me. "And oh, Amelia, Kenny and Ruston are absolutely lovely! They've promised to visit me in Kansas City this spring!"

I laugh. I'll need to buy my friends an expensive bottle of wine for whatever sweet-talking they did with Mom. As my gaze sweeps the room to find them talking to Seb and Bea, I do a double take. Bea doesn't have Fluff with her. I think it's a first to see her without her support cat.

When I turn back to Mom, her eyes are a little wet. It might be because her wrist hurts, but I ignore that unkind thought and hug her. We don't have to be close, but . . . I do want a relationship with my mother.

Life, after all, is too short to hold grudges.

Chapter Nineteen

THAT'S WHAT I WANT FOR CHRISTMAS

Travis

"I'd like to invite Travis and Amelia to the floor for their first dance," Addie announces. I stand and pull my wife's—my wife's! —chair back, then take her hand.

"Have you guessed the song I chose?" I ask her as I lead her around the table. The dance floor isn't huge, but plenty big enough for the two of us, especially after I pull her into my arms.

She shakes her head, eyes bright and cheeks flushed from the wine and, I hope, the excitement of the evening. The reception has gone great. Perfectly, I might even say. Which is a freaking holiday miracle at this point.

"It's a Christmas song," I say. "Not a well-known popular one, but one my mom used to listen to back when I was a kid."

I kiss her cheek and swing her slowly around as the song starts. Then I hold her close and sing the lyrics softly to her, about how what I want for Christmas is to love and be loved by her. Amelia closes her eyes and lays her head against my chest. Everything and everyone around us fades away.

This moment has been years in the making, but like I tell the anxious parents of pregnant pets, these things sometimes take their own time.

In that circle of light in the dining room of the Lazy Dog Ranch one December night in Colorado, surrounded by the love and support of our family and friends and even our pets, what matters now is that Amelia is mine and I'm hers.

Finally.

Epilogue

Doug

Our humans finally get back from the place with the dogs, the cats, the smells of delicious food cooking that made my stomach growl, and the snake wrapped around the tall indoor tree that smelled like dog pee. They turn the fireplace on, take us out, change their fur, and smush their faces together for a long time.

When they move to the bed, laughing and whispering, Daisy and I figure it's time to climb in our crate for the night. But as I curl up beside her, I spot the metal circles around our humans' fingers, the circles that a wise old pug once told me meant that they love each other very much. The same way our humans put harnesses and sweaters on us when they love *us*.

I turn to Daisy with a triumphant grin, and in the language we've always shared, I tell her:

"We did it. We did it all."

THE END

It all started with a girl, a boy, and a pug named Doug.
Get the exclusive Love & Pets prequel for FREE!

Like fantasy romance? Read the Brilliant Darkness series by A.G. Henley!
Get the Brilliant Darkness series here!

Like young adult thrillers? Read Double Black Diamond: A Nicole Rossi Thriller by A.G. Henley!
Get Double Black Diamond here!

Read Next

The Brilliant Darkness Series Box Set

The truth can't always be seen.

Seventeen-year-old Groundling, Fennel, is Sightless. She's never been able to see her lush forest home, but she knows its secrets. She knows how the shadows shift when she passes under a canopy of trees. She knows how to hide in the cool, damp caves when the Scourge comes. She knows how devious and arrogant the Groundlings' tree-dwelling neighbors, the Lofties, can be. And she's always known this day would come—the day she faces the Scourge alone.

Read the complete Brilliant Darkness series by USA Today bestselling author AG Henley for less than purchasing each book individually, and find out why readers call this series, **"My new favorite!"**, **"Darkly romantic"**, and **"A captivating story and fascinating world."**

The Brilliant Darkness series:

1. The Scourge
2. The Keeper: A Brilliant Darkness Story
3. The Defiance
4. The Gatherer: A Brilliant Darkness Story
5. The Fire Sisters

The Scourge

Chapter One

I duck out of the storeroom and into the main cavern, stepping carefully across the uneven floor. My fingers ache from being trailed along the frigid stone walls for hours. Rubbing my hands together to generate warmth has all the effect of kindling a fire with chips of ice.

My footfalls echo in the stillness as I move down the passage toward the mouth of the cave, counting my paces as I go. The sun pours in, diluting the darkness. I can barely tell light from dark, but I know I'm almost out when I hear Eland's voice. He never ventures in alone. He hates the caves almost as much as he fears the Scourge.

"Let's go, Fennel," he calls. "The celebration's about to start, and I'm starving. There's roasted boar and fresh bread, bean and potato stew, blackberry pie—"

I laugh. "Is your stomach all you think about?"

"No, I think about lots of other things."

"Really? Like what?" I reach out toward his voice.

Eland's hand, grimy from digging up vegetables and herbs in the garden, finds mine. Grimy or not, the warmth is a relief. "Like how we'll trounce the Lofties in the competitions tomorrow."

I can't help smiling at his confidence. This is his first year to compete. He and the other twelve-year-old boys have talked of little else for weeks. Everyone looks forward to the Summer Solstice celebration for the feast, the dancing, and the chance to beat the Lofties—with spear and knife, if not bow and arrow. It's a highlight of the year, so different from the solemn Winter Solstice when the Exchange takes place.

The shadows shift as we pass under the canopy of trees. I wrap my hand around Eland's sapling-thin arm—roots and creeping weeds on the forest floor have sent me sprawling more often than I want to remember. We reach the clearing, the heart of our community, where a bonfire sizzles and sputters to life. People shout to each other as they make their way down the paths from the gardens and the water hole, their work done for the day. The luscious fragrance of gardenia winds through the air. Someone must have strung garlands as decorations.

Our home, like those of all the other Groundlings, nestles into the embrace of the towering greenheart trees circling the clearing. Eland pushes open the door of our shelter. Aloe, my foster mother and his natural mother, calls to us from inside.

"Come in here, Eland ... are you presentable? Comb your hair and be sure you clean the muck out of those fingernails. Fennel? Did you finish in the caves?"

I move to Aloe's side, where I know her outstretched arm will be, and take her hand in mine. Her skin is weathered but warm, like the surface of the enormous clay cooking pot in the clearing that never quite cools off. She smells of rosemary, from working in the herb garden, and something else I can only liken to the scraps of pre-Fall metal we sometimes come across in the forest.

"There's plenty of blankets and firewood, but we could probably use more salt meat," I tell her.

"We can store what's left of the boar after the celebration. We're fortunate the hunting party came across such a large one, and so near to home. The Council is pleased."

"When will they meet?"

"Soon. Sable and Adder want to perform the ceremony before the Lofties arrive."

Aloe will join the Groundling Council of Three tonight. One more reason to look up to her. Aloe is the most capable person I know. I was given to her as an infant to foster because she's Sightless, like me. She taught me to rely on myself first, and others only when absolutely necessary. Her guidance made my childhood much easier.

"Can't we come, Mother?" Eland says through clenched teeth. He's combing his hair, but it sounds like he's stripping the bark off a dead tree. "We want to see you accepted into the Three."

"Try not to make yourself bald, my love. And no, you can't. The acceptance is private, like all meetings of the Council." She kisses him, and her stick taps away toward the door.

"Congratulations, Aloe," I say. "We're proud of you."

"As I am of you both, my children. I'll meet you later, at the celebration."

Eland follows her out to check on the preparations, mucky fingernails forgotten. The scent of burning wood and roasting meat rushes into my nose and throat as he opens the door. It makes my mouth water. Animated voices burst through the clearing like startled birds.

I wash my face and hands with the water from our basin and sit on my bed, a low wooden pallet along the wall. I work my fingers through my hair—the same color as the fertile soil of the gardens, I'm told—and a thrill runs through me. I wonder if I'll be asked to dance tonight.

When a boy asks a girl my age, seventeen years, to dance at the Summer Solstice celebration, it usually means he's singled her out as his partner—for life, not just for the dance. My best friend, Callistemon, is convinced Bear will ask me. I'm not so sure. We've all been friends since childhood, and I haven't noticed any change in how he treats me. Calli says she can tell by the way he looks at me now. I laugh, but it bothers me that I can't see what she means for myself.

I don't know if Bear will ask me, and I'm even less sure what I'll say if he does. He's courageous and loyal, and there's no boy I like better. But ... maybe I'm just not ready to partner. Aloe didn't until she was a few years older. I don't really remember her partner, Eland's father, but people say they were happy.

I take special care with my hair all the same, twisting it into thin braids here and there, and tucking in the fresh wild flowers Aloe left by the basin. It can't hurt to look my best.

Eland crashes back through the door to fetch me, and I follow him out. The bonfire blazes now. The heat isn't necessary on such a warm evening, but a fire makes everything more festive. A group across the clearing from our shelter howls with laughter. Hearing the musicians warming up sends another jolt of anticipation through my body. Calli calls to me as Eland scampers off. She's talking before I even sit down.

"You look so pretty, Fenn. I love how you fixed your hair! I'm so nervous ... do you think anyone will ask us to dance? Well, I already know who's going to ask you."

I cringe. "*Shh*, he might hear you."

"Relax. He's way over by the roasting pit. Oh, who do you think will ask me? What if no one does? I'd be so embarrassed ... but I hope it's not Cricket. He's so serious. And short."

"There are worse things than being short and serious ... like being chronically unwashed." We both snicker. Hare, one of the boys our age, never picked up the habit of bathing regularly.

"No danger there. I heard Hare's asking Clover," Calli says.

"Clover? Really?" She's been saying she won't partner with anyone since we were about seven.

"That's what I heard," she says, and I don't doubt her. Gossip is rampant.

More people enter the clearing now, greeting each other with high spirits. Calli and I stand when Rose stops to say hello. Her tinkly voice reminds me of the wind chimes we made as children using pebbles and bits of shell dredged up from the water hole. We touch her tidy round belly, which is as firm and warm as a healthy newborn's cheek. Not long ago, Rose and Jackal exchanged bonding bands, the leather strips partners wear around their arms as a physical sign of their commitment to each other. Soon after, they announced she was expecting and due when the trees finally shed their leaves. It's a good time of year to give birth. The baby will be too young to be taken up in the Exchange, this winter at least.

"She's so lucky," Calli says as Jack leads Rose off. "They seem so happy."

"For now," I say.

"I can't stand the suspense! I want someone to ask me to dance and get it over with!"

"Why? It's not like you have your heart set on partnering with someone in particular."

"I don't want to be the only one not asked, you know?"

I do know, although I think I'm more willing to suffer the humiliation of not being asked than to agree to partner for life with whoever might feel like asking me today.

"Here comes *Beaarr*," Calli says, wickedness in her voice, "looks like he's bringing you an offering." I elbow her.

"I snuck a few slices of boar for you both. Be careful; it's still hot," Bear says, his voice a low and familiar rumble.

I blow on the meat and then test it out with a nibble. Delicious. Not many large animals are left on the forest floor, and hunting them is always a risk because of the Scourge, so boar's a special treat. The muscular texture and rich, smoky flavor evoke cherished memories of past feasts: music, dancing, rare carefree moments.

"Maybe this is your old friend, Fenn," Calli says, like she does every time we eat boar. I smile and agree, like I do every time she says it.

I was almost killed by an animal when we were about ten. We were playing hide-and-seek in the forest, and I was the seeker. Aloe made me memorize every path, bush, and tree in the area around our homes, so most of the time I could pinpoint where I was when we played. But on this day I was lost. As I wandered around hunting a familiar landmark, I heard what sounded like a gigantic boar snorting and charging toward me through the underbrush. Just before the animal reached me it squealed as if in pain and ran back the way it had come, leaving me shaking but alive. I don't know what caused it to turn around.

"So Bear, who will you ask to dance tonight?" Calli teases.

"Better worry about who's asking you," Bear says. "From what I hear, Cricket's got you in his sights. That is, if he can see you from way down there."

We laugh at Calli's tortured moans.

"Don't you think it's unfair that only boys can ask girls to dance?" I say. "Why can't it be the girls' choice for a change?"

"*Tradition*," Calli says, in a high-pitched imitation of our teacher, Bream's, voice.

"Our *traditions* protect us from the Scourge," Bear says in the same voice. He leans closer to me, the smell of toasted wood clinging to his hair, and murmurs, "Who would you ask, if you had the choice?"

I chew a mouthful of meat to buy time. A voice bellows right above us, saving me from having to answer. It's Calli's father, Fox. He isn't one of the Three, but he's sure to be eventually, when Sable or Adder either die or become too infirm to do their duties.

"Ready for tomorrow, Bear?" Fox sounds like he's had one too many cups of the spiced wine.

"I still want to know," Bear whispers to me, before pushing himself to his feet. "We'll do our best," he says to Fox. "I hear the Lofties have a new crop of—"

"Rumors, rumors," Fox says. "Pay no attention. We have the advantage, as always."

Soon they're debating which shape of knife is best to use in the fights, or what spear grip will produce the most accurate throw. Other men join them to strategize. Some of the younger children run around us, shrieking with excitement. I lean back on my hands, enjoying the sounds of the people enjoying themselves.

"Fenn?" Calli says.

"*Hmm?*"

"Aren't you scared?"

I know what she's asking about. Now that Aloe joined the Three, I'll take over her duty and collect the water for our people when the Scourge comes again. I spend hours in the caves every day stocking the storeroom with supplies and food so we're ready, but we'll still need water. I shrug, feigning confidence. "Aloe says protection is the gift of our Sightlessness."

Which may be true, but I'm still terrified. The sighted say the creatures' bodies are open in patches, weeping pus and thick, dark blood. Their deformed faces are masks of horror. They roam the forests, reeking of festering flesh, consuming anything living. People who survive the attacks become flesh-eaters themselves. Death is better.

I'm supposed to be safe from the Scourge, like Aloe, but I haven't been tested. I will be soon. To hear the agony of their hunger, smell their disease, feel their hot breath on my skin ... the idea fills me with dread and loathing. But Aloe has never shown her fear to others, and neither will I.

"I won't be completely alone, anyway. I'll have my Keeper," I say. Calli snorts. The Lofties say the Keeper's job is to kill flesh-eaters and deter other fleshies—our nickname for the Scourge—from getting too close to me. But everyone knows the Keeper's really there to ensure the Lofties get their share of the water while the Scourge is here. Secretly I'm just happy *someone* will be with me, even if it's a Lofty in the trees. "Aloe insists her Keeper was important."

"*Self*-important," Calli mutters. "And devious. Don't trust them, Fenn." We all know the fate of Groundlings who cross Lofties. They're found with arrows in their chests. Or in their backs. It doesn't happen often, but it happens.

There's a rustling, more deliberate than the wind, in the leafy branches above our heads. I sit up.

"What is it?" Calli asks.

"The Lofties are here."

The talking and shrieking abruptly cease. The clearing is silent except for the chattering of the fire. Fox finally speaks, sounding stiff and formal—and more sober than I expected.

"Welcome. Please join us."

The woman who answers sounds equally uncomfortable. "Thank you. We brought food to contribute to the feast."

"Our Council hasn't arrived yet ... so I'll just say a few words in their absence." Fox clears his throat and continues in his best speechmaking voice—the one Calli and I have heard many times when we were in trouble. "Groundlings and Lofties come together once a year on this day to feast, to dance, and to engage in friendly competition." I smile as some of the boys quietly scoff at the word *friendly*. "The Summer Solstice celebration is a reminder that every year given to us since the Fall of Civilization is a blessing, something for us to treasure. It's a time to reflect on the year that has passed, and to anticipate the year that will be. We honor those who came before us, our elders, many of whom gave their lives to ensure we would have a future." He pauses. "And we offer a prayer of protection for those who come after us—our children, and our children's children. May they always be safe from the Scourge."

The Lofty woman responds to Fox's traditional words of welcome with their customary response. "We appreciate the hospitality of our Groundling neighbors. We too pray for peace and protection, and for a year of prosperity for all forest-dwellers."

A respectful silence follows, promptly broken by Bear's less-than-respectful whisper that the Lofties will need a prayer of protection tomorrow. Calli giggles.

"What are the Lofties doing?" I ask as conversations around the fire slowly start up again.

Bear answers. "Standing around, looking like they'd rather be anywhere else. As usual."

"It's kind of sad. They come to the Summer Solstice celebration every year, but they never seem to have any fun," Calli says.

"They should invite us up to their little nests if they aren't comfortable down here," Bear says. "Wouldn't kill 'em."

"Why do we bother to celebrate together, when we all keep to ourselves?" I ask. "We can do that anytime."

"*Tradition,*" Calli and Bear intone.

"Maybe it's time for a new tradition." I stand up, shaking out my skirt. "Where are they, exactly?"

"Over by my family's shelter," Calli says. "What are you doing, Fenn?"

Finding out who will be in those trees when the Scourge comes. I weave around the clusters of people, listening for voices I don't recognize. But I smell the Lofties before I hear them—the intense, slightly bitter resin of their homes, the greenheart trees.

"Welcome." My voice sounds too loud in my ears. "I'm Fennel. I'll be taking Aloe's place collecting water for our communities when the Scourge returns."

The Groundlings behind me fall silent again, their stares heavy on my shoulders. A Lofty speaks, his voice deep and gravelly.

"Fennel, it's Shrike. Has Aloe joined the Council then?" Shrike is Aloe's Keeper. She doesn't talk about him much, but I've always gotten the sense she thinks well of him.

"She was accepted this evening. She should be here soon." I worry the pocket of my dress with my fingers. "Shrike, could I ... I'd like to meet my Keeper."

There's silence, then someone moves toward me, crunching leaves under their feet.

"This is Peregrine," Shrike says.

I hold out my hand. It stays extended in front of me for what seems a very long time. I think of myself frozen that way, a welcoming statue found years in the future by someone who happens across the clearing. Embarrassed, but determined not to show it, I thrust my hand out even further.

A hand finally brushes mine. I can tell it belongs to a man. There are calluses on the ends of his long fingers. This Lofty smells different from the others, more like ... honeysuckle. I liked playing around the honeysuckle in the garden as a child, avoiding the preoccupied bees and soaking in the sweet, sunny scent. It's the fragrance of summer.

"Hello, Fennel."

I'm surprised. I pictured my Keeper middle-aged, like Shrike, but this Lofty doesn't sound much older than me. And while his hand is rough, his voice isn't. It's quiet, almost melodious. More like the calls of the warblers that wake us each morning than the predatory screech of the falcon he's named for. All the Lofty men are named for birds, while the women have ridiculous names like Sunbeam, Dewdrop, and Mist.

"Though I don't wish the Scourge to return," Aloe says from behind me, "they will. It's good that you've met."

"Congratulations on your acceptance into the Three," Shrike says. "You'll serve your community well."

"Thank you," she says.

Aloe's voice is different, gentler, the voice she reserves for

Eland. She has a bond with this Lofty. I wonder if I'll have a similar bond with my rough-handed, soft-voiced Keeper.

"So," I say to Peregrine, "were you chosen because you're a good hunter? Aloe says Shrike is deadly, as deadly as she's ever known a man to be."

"I can use a bow and arrow."

"Ha, don't let him fool you. Peree's one of our best archers. We're counting on him tomorrow." Shrike sounds proud, like he's talking about his own son. Maybe he is. We don't know much about the Lofties.

Fox's voice booms across the clearing. "Come, eat, and let the dancing begin! We have some anxious boys here, waiting to find out if the girls they've had their eye on for the past year will dance with them." The crowd laughs, even a few of the Lofties. People all around the fire begin to talk normally again, and the music starts up. I'm relieved that the collective attention seems to have turned away from me.

I smile politely at my Keeper. "I'm sure we'll meet again, Peregrine, like Aloe said."

"Call me Peree. Everyone does."

I nod. "My friends call me Fenn."

The music starts up. I should go. Bear, or someone else, may be waiting to dance with me. Whether I want to or not. I turn away ... and a mad idea grabs me.

Ask the Lofty to dance.

I hesitate. Is Aloe still nearby? Can she hear us? She's one of the Three now, tasked with managing our complicated relationship with the Lofties. There's no rule against dancing with them, but that's only because no one has ever tried. Aloe—not to mention the rest of my people—might be furious with me. I decide I don't care. At least I'll have made my own choice.

"Peree? Would you like to dance?" He doesn't say anything. I bite my bottom lip. "You know, dance? I'm not bad, really. I won't even step on your feet much."

"Lofties and Groundlings don't dance together."

"Why not?"

He's quiet again. "No idea. Tradition, I guess." I half expect him to say it in Bream's voice.

I hold my hand out, palm up this time, challenging him.

I never get an answer. Shrill birdcalls rip through the air—Lofty warning calls. The music dies, and for a moment the clearing is quiet. Then the screaming starts.

The Scourge is here.

Read The Brilliant Darkness box set

The PPP (The Pandemonium of Pets Playlist)

Check out the playlist of holiday songs I curated to go along with *The Pandemonium of Pets*.

Listen, read, and enjoy!

https://open.spotify.com/playlist/oEUQRCT5ci8htTqIRDAarL

Acknowledgments

If you began reading the Love & Pets series when I published the first book, *The Problem with Pugs*, then I owe you a great big thank you for sticking with it and an apology. This seventh book has been a long time coming.

I decided to write a pet related romantic comedy on a whim back in 2017, PUGS was published in spring 2018, and then our family moved cross-country. I finally got back to writing the rest of the series in 2019 and 2020. And now, here we are at the end of a turbulent year.

At the start of the pandemic, I thought this might be a terrible year to write light, humorous, sweet romances. Who would want to read those amidst all the serious issues we all have faced?

But you, my readers, proved me wrong. You've embraced the series, enjoyed it, reviewed it, and even let me know once in a while that the books were torchlights in what has been, at times, a very dark year. Thank you.

Many thanks to the Henley Huddle, my review team. I would not have had such great launches the last year and a half without you and your work reading the book early and providing prompt, honest reviews. I'm grateful to Lorie Humpherys for her ridiculously quick proofreading services, to Najla Qamber and her team at Najla Qamber Designs for the adorable, fun covers of these books, and to Kathy Azzolina and Terri White for always cheering me on from afar.

To my family, thank you always. You're my sounding boards, complaint boxes, and not-so-secret Valentines. I'm so fortunate that you're mine.

Also by A. G. Henley

The Love & Pets Series (Sweet Romantic Comedy)

Love, Pugs, and Other Problems: A Love & Pets Prequel Story

The Problem with Pugs

The Trouble with Tabbies

The Downside of Dachshunds

The Lessons of Labradors

The Predicament of Persians

The Conundrum of Collies

The Pandemonium of Pets: A Love & Pets Christmas Romance

The Love & Pets Series Box Set: Books 1 - 3

Nicole Rossi Thrillers (Young Adult)

Double Black Diamond

The Brilliant Darkness Series (Young Adult Fantasy)

The Scourge

The Keeper: A Brilliant Darkness Story

The Defiance

The Gatherer: A Brilliant Darkness Story

The Fire Sisters

The Brilliant Darkness Boxed Set

Novellas (Young Adult Fantasy)

Untimely

Featured in *Tick Tock: Seven Tales of Time*

Basil and Jade

Featured in *Off Beat: Nine Spins on Song*

The Escape Room

Featured in *Dead Night: Four Fits of Fear*

About the Author

A.G. Henley is a *USA Today* bestselling author of novels and stories in multiple genres including thrillers, romantic comedies, and fantasy romances. The first book in her young adult Brilliant Darkness series, *The Scourge*, was a Library Journal Self-e Selection and a Next Generation Indie Book Award finalist. She's also a clinical psychologist, but she promises not to analyze you . . . much.

Find her at:
aghenley.com
Email Aimee